HOW TO GET ALONG

with

WOMEN

HOW TO GET ALONG

with

WOMEN

SHORT STORIES

ELISABETH DE MARIAFFI

Invisible Publishing

Halifax & Toronto

Library and Archives Canada Cataloguing in Publication

De Mariaffi, Elisabeth, 1973-
    How to get along with women : stories / Elisabeth de
Mariaffi.

Short stories.
ISBN 978-1-926743-26-4

        I. Title.

PS8609.E2357H69 2012   C813'.6   C2012-904844-5

Cover & Interior designed by Megan Fildes

Typeset in Laurentian and Slate by Megan Fildes
With thanks to type designer Rod McDonald

Printed and bound in Canada

Invisible Publishing
Halifax & Toronto
www.invisiblepublishing.com

We acknowledge the support of the Canada Council for the Arts which last
year invested $20.1 million in writing and publishing throughout Canada.

Invisible Publishing recognizes the support of the Province of Nova Scotia
through the Department of Communities, Culture & Heritage. We are
pleased to work in partnership with the Culture Division to develop and
promote our cultural resources for all Nova Scotians.

This one is for Nora and for Desmond

DANCING ON THE TETHER

1.

Zelda comes up the laneway on her bicycle, going slow because it's dusty and because sometimes a pickup pulls out quick, the driver not expecting anyone to be walking or cycling way out here. She can see Tim about halfway down the drive working on the Ranger, his head down in the engine and she leans her bike against the fence and takes her schoolbag, which was hanging across her chest for the ride, and lifts it over her head and lets it hang from just one shoulder and walks up behind him.

I need to ask you a favour.

He doesn't look up. He says, Pass me that screwdriver there, babe.

Zelda hands him the screwdriver. Seriously. Tim.

He pulls his head and shoulders out from under the hood and turns, flips his chin at her.

Take your shirt off.

Tim. She steps toward him a little and rocks back and forth on her heels.

What?

I need something.

So do I, baby.

I need you to do something for me.

He puts the screwdriver down, leans his head down too. Lifts up his eyes to look at Zelda. You know you're no fun.

He's squinting. There's a lot of cloud but it's bright cloud. Zelda doesn't answer right away and he picks up the screwdriver again and goes back to work on the V belt. There's some wind and the hood shakes a little, propped up there. Tim stays bent over. Zelda wonders if the wind were strong enough, could the hood fall down on his shoulders.

Tim lived with them, Zelda and Mary, for six whole months back in the winter and spring. He used to take Max for walks and he let Zelda tag along and showed her how to get Max to drop one stick before you throw another. He got up and made macaroni and cheese for breakfast when Mary was out working late the night before and once when he was rolling up a joint on the kitchen table, Zelda knocked over a glass of milk and soaked his rolling papers and he didn't even lose his shit.

Zelda says, I need you to drive me up north.

Fuck. Gimme that impact driver.

She finds it and gives it over.

I want to see where I was born.

Who knows where you were born, Tim says. He strips the belt out nice and clean, tosses it down, reaches back for the new one. Zelda picks it up and hands it to him. She doesn't say anything for a while. Tim's shoulders rock a little.

Tim.

You know I'm not even fucking your mom anymore. Go ask someone else. Ask Ray.

Ray's a jackass, Zelda says. That makes Tim feel okay and he brings a greasy hand up to rub his beard and hide it.

Ray brings over these big cheap cowboy steaks and pretends like they're something good, Zelda says. Mary can't even stand him half the time. She just needs someone around to, I don't know.

I know, Tim says. I know what she needs him for.

They stand there a minute with Tim still leaning under the hood but he looks at her and his hand drops and he bounces the impact driver against his thigh a few times.

Mary says Thunder Bay.

Screwdriver.

Zelda gives it to him. His shoulders give a last hard shudder. He straightens up and stretches his neck to the side, reaches for the prop and lets the hood fall back into place.

What do you really want to go up to Thunder Bay for?

I'll fuck you, Tim. If you take me.

Tim throws his tools into the box and he latches it and turns around and points a finger at her. No you won't. You say you will but you won't.

I guess.

You guess.

You're just too old for me, Tim.

They walk around the back of the house and up onto the porch. He has a big wooden table up there under the overhang and he slides the toolbox under the bench and they sit down. He takes a booklet of Zig-Zag out of his shirt pocket and raps the end of it against the tabletop and Zelda opens up her bag and takes out her stuff.

So? Zelda says.

So what? You got any tobacco, or just that shit?

Take me driving, Tim, Zelda says. You love my shit.

She'd been down to Turkey Point with Lorna Gallant and some boys they know. This was a few weeks earlier. One of the boys had a sky blue Impala and they parked it at the bottom of Ferris Street and went and sat around on the shore and let the wind push at their shoulders. Mary closes the bar on Wednesday and Thursday nights, so she doesn't notice if Zelda comes home late. Even if the school calls to say Zelda never showed up, Mary doesn't answer the phone. She turns it off so she can get some sleep.

It was maybe the last really good day. The rocks were all hot to touch, but the air off the lake was sharp and getting colder. Lorna wanted her sweater from the car. Zelda lay back and let one of the boys pile pebbles into her belly button. They were talking about music. When she saw that Lorna had gone up to where they'd parked, she rolled over and stood up and followed her. For God's sake, she said, Don't just leave me there. These weren't even boys they particularly liked.

They came back down to the water together and took off their shoes and socks and stuck their feet in and played around, wringing their hands and making a lot of exaggerated talk about how icy it was. Their toes got blue, wading, and when they came out the sand was wet and caked onto their feet and they didn't have a towel to clean them with, so they had to wait before they could put their shoes back on and this made them even colder and they laughed louder than ever. One of the boys had brought some beer and they made a fire on the beach and pried off the bottle caps with a penknife. Zelda said she knew a girl who'd done the same thing using her mouth instead of a knife and broke her front tooth. The boy with the pebbles put his arm around Lorna and started singing a song he knew about being drunk in New York City, but he hadn't brought a guitar or anything. When the sun started to go down there was an argument about leaving.

In the car on the way home, Zelda pulled Lorna into the back seat so they could ride together, and they slung their legs over each other and took turns braiding each other's hair. The boys slouched up front and played with the radio and rolled cigarettes. There was a Perly's Ontario mapbook, dirty on the floor and after Lorna went to sleep, Zelda got herself busy looking at it.

Thunder Bay is about the farthest you can go without leaving the province. You drive all the way up the number six to Tobermory, then you hop a boat to Manitoulin. The boat is called the *Chi Chi Maun*. On the other side of the island there's no boat, just a road that cuts over bits and pieces of water until you hit real land and all that big space between towns. The towns called Spanish, Blind River, Marathon, Wild Goose.

Tim gets up and takes the bag of pot from Zelda. My fee, he says. He goes inside for a minute. When he comes back out he's wearing a plaid shirt and carrying a pack of Djarum Black.

Cloves'll punch a hole in your lung, he tells her. Lighting up her smoke.

Zelda thinks about that and pulls hard on the clove. The buzz comes up through her nose like something sharp, horseradish, and she shakes her head and sniffs and feels the smoke settle into her chest.

She roasted a rabbit once, the week before, and was surprised by the range of organs left by the butcher, tidily laid out in the cavity. The lungs had been something spongy, only light. Like mousse, Zelda thinks. Or meringue, before you bake it.

2.

Mary reckons up. There was the incident with Max. That, and whether or not they could now be expected to recover. After she got Zelda calm and in bed, Mary tried to talk to Ray about it. He was down in the dark, watching some sitcom rerun and drinking from a bottle of scotch. He set the bottle on the floor next to his armchair and Mary sat in the chair opposite, half-watching the show, half-thinking how to say something without getting to Ray, getting his hackles up. Ray talked to her but looked at the screen and reached down for the bottle, unscrewed the cap, poured and replaced the cap, all without moving his eyes.

You always make it so I look bad, Ray said. You always make me the bad guy.

That's not true, Ray. Mary's voice slow and even. Kind, but not too kind: a mix of tenderness and remorse. Important that nothing sound like confrontation.

What I said was the opposite of that. That he's just a dog and it's my fault, you know, because I didn't train him, but there you go. He chews shit and you can rub his nose in it, but it won't pay you in the end, to get Zelda so upset, do you see that? She had a blue and white pack of cigarettes down in her lap and she opened and closed the lid without looking.

It was after two. The whole ordeal had gone on for an hour, with Zelda near hysterics and Mary holding onto her and then the dog whimpering in the kitchen for nearly another hour after that. They'd come in from the car, Ray already in a black mood—Zelda after Mary's attention all night at the arena—and they found the mess and Ray took off his belt. A lot, a lot just to hold Zelda back, and Mary's whole body cold with it. Not crying, just cold and sick. And then Zelda finally asleep and Mary wanting only to lie down on the kitchen floor herself with the dog, or to bring Max with her to Zelda's room and curl up in bed, curve her body against Zelda's with the dog down at their feet.

If they hadn't come home, if Ray had been working; if she'd been working. Ray had his own place still. If she'd held his hand back and not Zelda's.

Mary looked at Ray and thought about whether or not she could go upstairs. Was he likely to follow her up or just keep drinking here until he passed out. The key is to get the nod. Something between forgiveness and permission. You don't feel safe until you get that.

Is Ray gone, Zelda wants to know in the morning.

No. He's here. He's sleeping.

After Zelda leaves for school, late on her bicycle, Mary cleans the kitchen: every piece of cutlery, the burnt-milk saucepan, the bowls hardened with yesterday's cereal and Lipton noodles. Ray gets up and she can see he's still drunk. His eyes haven't changed. He might just as well be sitting in the dark basement again. She hears him get up and pee and then she hears the buzz of the electric razor and he stands in the bathroom and shaves his head clean. When he comes out to the kitchen he says, Hey Max. Hey boy, we're pals, right, and the dog flattens his ears and lies down and rolls on the floor at his feet. Ray looks up at Mary with his dead eyes and says nothing.

Then: Don't look at me like that. He jams his feet down into his boots and pushes hard enough at the screen that he may as well snap it. The house stinks. She walks around opening up the windows and drags the vacuum upstairs so she can get rid of Ray's black hair lying in a spray all over the bathroom floor, but she doesn't plug it in. She goes into

Zelda's room and pulls a red hoodie out of the drawer and puts on her jeans and drums her hands against her thighs and calls out so the dog will come. She wants to see how he's walking. She closes up all the windows again.

For a week she and Zelda were on their own, Ray up in Walkerton nailing shingles. They got down to making dinner together, Zelda laying a rabbit out in the roasting pan and Mary carving potatoes into little balls and rolling them in parsley. At least with Tim there weren't fights. A pothead and a partier, but he held his job and liked to cook pancakes on Saturday mornings. They didn't have much to say to each other. He liked the dog. He sat and watched Mary read the paper with the sunlight warming her feet on the white couch.

Max comes over now and Mary leashes him up and then she locks the door and they start down the street. When they come to the corner she stops a moment and looks over at the market. There's a few people huddled outside, drinking coffee from styrofoam cups with their collars wrapped high around their necks, and they're smoking cigarettes and she remembers how sometimes on a cold day smoking can make you feel better.

Mary! one of them yells, a guy she serves at the bar. He doesn't have a name. His name is jack-and-coke.

Her hands are in her pockets already, keeping warm, so she knows she doesn't have any money for coffee or for cigarettes, and instead of crossing the street she turns Max left and they walk off down Powell and toward the river. It's a long walk. When they get to where the trail opens up she takes Max into the woods and they go through where it's muddy, following tire tracks left by a few mountain bikes earlier in the day. The sky is grey and bright and heavy. Max pulls on his lead. There's a slap down along the water and

Mary looks up and sees the ass end of a beaver disappear under the surface and Max whines and she realizes he must have been watching it for some time.

They come out into a little clearing where the bikers have patched together a few ramps by digging out the hollows around tree roots. Off to one side there's a pile of old liquor bottles lying under a tree and Max pulls to go over for a better smell. A thin path branches off the clearing near the bottles and Mary gives it a look to see if it's wide enough for them to follow without Max getting full of burrs. There's another, smaller pile of bottles and some other junk as well, a few old rags of clothing, some cracked plastic toys, a baby's cup. Mary lets her eyes follow the trunk into the branches, up to a mobile—forty or fifty pieces of dollar store ribbon, each dangling a fork or a knife or a spoon off the end, and set far enough apart so as not to get tangled in the wind. Every time the branches move, the cutlery ripples and Mary stands there awhile, watching this, and thinking how the stainless steel must have glinted back in the summer sun.

The beaver is gone. There's no sound, not even the wind or the rustle and clink of the mobile. She leads Max back out to the clearing and hooks his leash around a stump, then goes over to the first pile and crouches down and picks up a couple of Sauza bottles and throws them hard as she can into the woods. The leaves lift off the trees: there's a bunch of crows hiding out in the branches and they flap away, crying out. Mary's chest loosens a little and she picks up a few more bottles and throws them too. They explode over the other side of the clearing, all over the trail and the makeshift ramps, Max dancing on his tether and whining the whole time.

3.

They drive for about an hour and then Tim pulls over at a McDonald's and orders a Big Mac in the wrapper and he buys Zelda a Coke and an apple pie. They eat and he drives. Zelda sucks on her straw. It gets noisy against the crushed ice at the bottom of the cup and she tosses the whole thing down onto the truck floor—maybe this will get a rise out of him, but it doesn't. She kicks at the cup a little. Tim steers one-handed with a cd case flat and open between his knees. He pushes the disc into the player, snaps the case shut and tosses it down into the door pocket. Cranks up the volume. They're driving with the windows down.

It wouldn't be that much further just to take me where I'm going to, Zelda says, loud over the music. I'm going anyway. You got nothing else keeping you busy.

The road is clear and open ahead of them. 2:05 p.m. by the clock on the dash. Zelda adds an hour in her head, since a knob broke off back in the winter and Tim hasn't bothered to fix it forward after daylight savings. The air coming in the window doesn't do much to cool her. She might go to sleep.

Tim says, If you miss the six o'clock you'll be stuck overnight in Tobermory. That's as far as he'll take her. So he says.

She doesn't have a plan for after Manitoulin and Tim knows it. She doesn't say anything back. She leans out and looks to see if he's watching her, the tip of her sunglasses in the side mirror. He is. Her shoulders square and sharp. There's a line to her jaw that's like Mary. She rubs the plastic bracelet up and down her arm.

Empty road behind them and nobody in front either. She checks to make sure he's still looking. In the sky it's sun and no clouds, the scrub on the roadside burnt back flat.

Weather moves fast the further north you go, Tim says.

Someone laid an inukshuk out on the high median and it's the only thing there.

Zelda reaches down and unclips her seatbelt. The mechanism clicks and then she's up and over the gear shift and straddling him, her back against the steering wheel, his driving arm pinned under her body. The truck swings sharp across the median and then back toward the gravel shoulder.

Tim's foot hard on the brake.

Jesus Fuck Jesus!

His shoulder hits the door and Zelda goes out onto the road. He sits there a moment with his door wide open then kills the engine. Gets out and leans his hands on his knees.

He spits once.

Zelda pulls herself up, looks down hard at the painted yellow line, and walks toward him. She's got a sore shoulder and for a moment she stops and rubs it with one hand, but she can walk.

What the fuck! You threw me out in the ROAD!

The truck with two wheels on the shoulder. When Tim straightens up she draws back both arms and pushes hard against his chest and he takes a step or two backward.

What was that shit? What the fuck do you think you're doing?

If she was a boy he'd knock her down.

Zelda says, What if a fucking car had been behind us?

He looks behind them. Nothing on the road.

I don't need your help, she says.

When they get back in the truck Tim leans over and jams the tongue of Zelda's seatbelt hard into the buckle.

Ow, she says. She throws her leg up on the dash and taps with the toe of her boot on the windshield. He puts on the signal and pulls out. When they've gone fifteen miles or so, the Fifth Wheel comes up on the right and he puts the signal back on again.

I'm taking a piss, Tim says.

I'm coming, Zelda says. The two of them walk into the store to get the bathroom key. Zelda picks up a pack of Sesame Snaps.

I'm not buying you fucking candy.

You gotta buy something or they won't give you the key.

Tim smacks the package on the counter and digs around in his pocket for quarters. Zelda leans over and grabs the key to the men's. They go straight to the back of the store and Zelda opens up the door and holds it for Tim and then follows him through. He unzips. Zelda watches him peeing.

What'd you do that for? Tim says.

What.

Jump on me in the truck. He shakes off and zips up.

I love you Tim.

Fuck you Zelda.

Okay. I want to keep you. Maybe I can do something you like.

That's sick.

Tim. Zelda throws the taps on. Wash your hands, she says. Tim steps up to the sink and pushes her aside with one hand, not hard.

You got Ray.

He runs his hands under the water and turns the taps off.

Ray's doing fucking rails on the fucking kitchen table at night. Zelda steps sideways, clear of the paper towel dispenser, and hops up to sit on the sink.

And Tim, she says. He hits Max.

He hits the dog?

He beat him with a belt. We came home and he'd chewed up a patch cord and Ray went fucking nuts and took off his belt and beat him with it. He was screaming.

Tim turns away and rams the handle of the paper towel holder up and down a few times, then rips off a long sheet.

Ray was screaming?

Max was.

What did Mary do?

She was holding me back.

Jesus fucking Christ, Zelda.

I want to keep you, Tim.

The door handle rattles and from the outside a man yells Phyllis, you in there?!

Zelda jumps off the sink. She pulls her sweater over her head and throws her arms up around Tim's neck. She still has her t-shirt on and it lifts off the waistband of her jeans with her arms up high like that. She's not wearing a bra.

What do you weigh, Zelda, ninety pounds? Tim says. Her skinny legs and the ribs sticking out under her breasts. She tries kissing Tim's neck and he shakes her off a little.

Phyllis I said that you in there?!

It's not fucking Phyllis, fuckhead, Tim says and outside the man slumps off to try the next locked door.

Zelda pulls back and runs her hands under some water in the sink, then rubs them through Tim's beard. Her hands are warm and his wet beard feels good to her. She waits until she knows he's looking, pulls the front of her t-shirt up to the shoulder and holds it there.

4.

When Zelda gets home Mary is there, vacuuming in her purple slip. The slip is satin with black lace trim along the neckline and down at the hem, where it grazes Mary's thighs.

This place is a fuzz palace, she says. She has music on, and there's the noise of the vacuum and Mary singing along *This here's a story of Billy Joe and Bobbie Sue...* Zelda goes into the kitchen.

Slip is the wrong word. A slip is something you wear under clothes, under a suit, to prevent static cling. It goes with a blouse and a hat, gloves even. It goes under.

She goes to the fridge and pours herself a glass of half grape juice, half ginger ale and then gets out a spoon and adds a scoop of vanilla from the freezer. The ice cream has frost crystals over the top of it and Zelda has to dig down underneath to get to the part that's good. She takes her drink and sits down at the table.

It's really a nightie.

Mary comes into the kitchen and says, What am I, Susie Homemaker? and sits down too and Zelda lets her have a sip of her drink and then she gets up and makes Mary one, too, just the same except with more ice crystals in it. There's getting to be almost none of the good part left.

Zelda says, Ray coming over?

There's animal hair everywhere, Mary says. I could spend all day cleaning, and sit down for an hour and look at it all clean and by the end of the hour it would be like this again. Just like this.

If he comes, do you think he'll bring those steaks again? Because I might be vegetarian. I've been thinking about it. You know, because the only way to eat a steak is real rare, and that seems sacrificial. To me.

Do you think there's much point? Mary says.

To being vegetarian?

To cleaning up. To making the fake house.

Zelda brings her hands up to her face and combs her fingers through her hair. She gets the smell of the clove cigarette and Tim's truck and the McDonald's pie, his wet beard against her fingers.

I was thinking that if you change what goes in your body, then maybe change what it does, Zelda says.

Think it can go backwards? Mary says.

Like how? Zelda says. There's a little foamy cream down in the bottom of her glass, a bit of white froth that hasn't totally sunk into grape-colour. Where's Max? she says suddenly.

I locked him outside in the back. He was attacking the vacuum cleaner. He's okay. I took him for a long walk.

He's okay, Mary says again.

Her long hair hanging loose over one shoulder. She draws her leg up onto the chair and hugs her knee and lets her chin rest on it. She looks at Zelda.

Zelda sees Mary's top lip is stained purple from the drink, the same colour as the slip. Nightie. Whatever.

We could just move more, Zelda says. You could throw away the vacuum and whenever it gets too hairy in a place, we just vacate.

Vamoose, Mary says.

Can I let Max back in now?

Vacate, Mary says. I wonder.

15

KISS ME LIKE I'M THE LAST MAN ON EARTH

I met Asher Katz in the spring of 1984, when I was ten years old and he was already eleven. He came loping over the parking lot at my grandmother's condo on Bathurst Street, a shiny black condom machine hoisted on one shoulder and a toolbox in the other hand. He was wearing a Run DMC t-shirt and a yarmulke and his jeans were hemmed up high so his bony ankles stuck out. His father was the Vending Machine King of Lawrence West.

What do all these *alte Kakes* need with condoms? my grandmother said. We had just come in from Open Window bakery and she had a shopping cart with a caraway rye and nothing else in it. I spent all my Saturdays with her, grocery shopping and sitting around at her place while she gave voice lessons to adults who had regular jobs during the week.

It's for the laundry room, Asher said, and I pictured all my grandmother's old Jewish neighbours standing around in their underwear and girdles, helpless with boredom in front of the dryers. Location location location, Asher said.

My grandmother was probably the only gentile in that building. She was married to a Viennese Jew thirty years her senior and nailed a Mezuzah to her threshold so that no one would ask questions. Outside the condo she had an aggressive anxiety about being mistaken for a Jew that was left over from her days as a Hungarian refugee. Once when she was sitting on the Bathurst bus an old man pushed up his shirt sleeve and flashed her his Auschwitz tattoo.

Where is your number? the man said. She took this for a come-on and called him an old cocksucker.

I couldn't see a lot of difference between my grandmother and the other old ladies in that building: she baked the same cookies and spoke the same Yiddish-inflected German. She played mah-jongg on Wednesday afternoons. Inside the apartment there were only a few religious icons. On the shelf she had a velvet-covered pocket bible that had belonged to her mother and there was a rosary in her jewellery drawer. In the bathroom she had an electrified portrait of the Virgin Mary. Mary was peeling the flesh back from her ribcage like a cardigan. Inside glowed a tiny red lamp: her bleeding heart.

Because we were both kids and that building was adults-only, Asher and I fell in together almost defensively. He'd been working the machines since he was seven and made his rounds every Saturday like other kids with their paper routes. I don't remember anyone introducing us. The day we met, we all stood outside the elevators with both arrows, up and down, shining orange. When the doors opened, my grandmother went upstairs with a red-haired woman named Marijke Smirins and I followed Asher down to the laundry room. I stood under the machine and braced it with my shoulder while he used a plug-in drill to screw it to the wall.

Asher was a Latvian Jew. I knew about Latvians because my public school downtown hosted Heritage Language.

Every Saturday and all summer long, the teacher parking lot filled up with beaten-down old Volvos and VWs and Pontiacs bearing the SVEIKS bumper sticker. Latvians, my father said low in his throat whenever we saw one of these cars driving down Bayview Avenue, his voice a mix of disapproval and disbelief. He looked upon nationality as a matter of character. How could anyone could choose their heritage so poorly?

SVEIKS always looked to me like the kind of word that should be painted across the side of a Viking ship. It looks Swedish.

It means Latvia, my mother told me.

It means Hello, Asher said, tightening a bolt on the machine. Jesus. He was good at swearing in the way experience has shown me all Eastern Europeans are. He liked to bring the Messiah into it when he could. I thought it sounded dirty and ravenous coming from him. The way Asher smiled I could tell he would do it just to please me.

I asked him if he went to Heritage Language and he didn't even look up. I'm a Jew, he said. I don't go to Russian school. I go to Hebrew school.

You mean after school?

No, that's my school. Hebrew school.

My own family was ethnically Catholic at best. My parents ran their lives on very practical terms. Ours was a secular existence for the most part and I had only recently begun to understand that there were whole worlds outside of "Catholic" and "Jewish," the only two categories I'd ever had contact with. My Girl Guide troop met in the basement of Bethel Baptist church; once a year we paraded in on a Sunday morning to commemorate Lady Baden-Powell's birthday. After the service we ate tiny white-bread sandwiches with all the congregation ladies and one of the other girls told me she was United.

Is that Catholic? I asked. She frowned and bit into a deviled egg.

Asher's account of Glencairn Chabad was news to me: a religious school that replaced regular school.

Is it like French immersion?

The machine was on the wall now and Asher grabbed a corner of it and shook, to make sure it was fastened nice and tight.

No, he said.

But you learn Hebrew.

Yes.

And pray and stuff?

Yes.

So is it like Sunday school?

No.

Do you still have to do math?

Asher dropped his wrench back into the toolbox and snapped the lid.

It's like French immersion, he said.

I had gone to Hungarian school just once, at the Magyar Ház on St. Clair West. It was a dark room filled with rows of desks; in the desks, children traced stencils of the Hungarian alphabet. You had to follow the dotted lines to form the letters. That makes it sound as though the Hungarian alphabet is somehow its own thing, like Cyrillic or Kanji, but it's no different from the Latin alphabet I had already mastered in public school. What the dotted lines were really teaching was the kind of stylized, uniform cursive that every Hungarian kid is expected to learn: penmanship,

Soviet-style. My mother, seeing herself as progressive, was horrified at the thought of confining me to a dark room and the mindless drudgery of stencils.

We have so little good weather in this country! she said to my father. It was her way of saying that kids should be allowed to play outside after school. As a result my Hungarian cultural training was restricted to the banter and dirty language of Uncle Bug-Eye István, who came for lunch every second Sunday, and the occasional evening out at the Csárda, a supper club for Hungarians where my parents liked to go and listen to Transylvanian gypsies.

The Latvian school kids were not so lucky. From the ages of four to twelve, their Saturdays were consigned to Latvian Heritage—and its Language. It disturbed me to think of another child sitting at my public school desk, perhaps using my coloured pencils, perhaps even thinking of it as his own desk, while I took advantage of the precious little sun and fresh air that a country like Canada offered. While I rode my bicycle around and around our paved-over front yard, I was always half thinking about that Latvian kid sitting in my desk and what he might be up to. In grade three I made a koala bear out of papier mâché and got so worked up over its safety, vis-à-vis the Latvians, that my mother had to drive me to school on a Saturday morning to retrieve it.

She stood in the door holding my coat, while I walked across the classroom to the art table. The Latvian teacher stood there, too, with her arms at her sides. In my desk there was boy about three years younger than me. He was tracing a stencil. The art table was jammed with papier mâché animals. I grabbed my koala and hugged it against my hip. The Latvians looked at me. They didn't seem surprised to see a public school kid on a craft rescue mission. A girl in the front row sucked on the tip of her blond braid.

In the car I looked down at the koala in my lap. It was about a foot-and-a-half long with a blotchy red mouth. I had spent days building it up with paste and newspaper, also spreading the paste over my arms and hands. When it dried, it made my skin look wrinkled, like I was old.

I wedged my fingernail up underneath the buttons and picked off the koala's eyes.

Russians, my mother said from the front seat.

From what Asher said, Glencairn Chabad sounded like those schools they made movies about in the 60s, like the Summerhill school or Waldorf, except instead of blonde hair and English accents the kids were all brunette and wore Star of David necklaces. I liked how everyone shared a common identity: the big white and blue flag, the special holidays, the packed-lunch sandwiches that all looked the same. In my own east-end neighbourhood, everybody had names like Fitzgerald or Mackenzie or Halliday or Jones, and they lived in brick houses with hamsters and guinea pigs or a wall of pet birds in cages. At my public school downtown, my best friend My Le was a Vietnamese girl who had lived the startling and delicious experience of watching a man's dangling legs get sliced off when her own refugee boat scraped up against another boat in the Saigon harbour.

It's not all the same, Asher said. There's orthodox kids and immigrants and Israelis, he said. There's fights at lunch. Some people live in Forest Hill.

I didn't know where Israel was so he hauled out a book of maps to show me. I told him how when we were driving up Bathurst Street, my Uncle Bug-Eye István liked to lean out the car window and yell, The Arabs are coming! The Arabs are coming! whenever he thought an old lady was driving too slow.

Asher wasn't more than an inch or two taller than me and he still had his little-boy skinniness, all ribcage and big teeth at odd angles, but he approached grown-ups with a balanced irreverence. Where I was normally never allowed to go even as far as the smelly garbage chute in the hallway by myself, somehow if I was with Asher, my grandmother was only too pleased to wash her hands of me. The two of us roamed the neighbourhood for hours, checking stock in Asher's machines and buying cheese danishes at Open Window. I liked to go to Lawrence Plaza and try on high heel shoes and make him sit and watch me hobble up and down the aisles at Shoe Company. He threw his legs over the side of the armchair and held his head in his hands. I'm so Christ-fucking bored, he said.

It was the closest we came to flirtation. We'd leave the plaza and walk down the street, kicking each other viciously. Because my grandmother's apartment was an opera studio on the weekends, we usually ended up back in Asher's basement.

Asher's house reminded me a little of mine. It was clean, without all the stuff lying around I saw in other people's houses. His parents liked antiques and, aside from the basement, there was no wall-to-wall carpeting, just rugs on a wood floor. In the kitchen there were some plates hanging on the walls, and in the living room a lot of black and white photographs of aunts and uncles and great-grandparents back in Russia. There was a dining room with a big table and a blue tablecloth and a menorah on the window ledge. I'd been to a Jewish wedding once and sat at the kids' table and remembered that the bride had worn a pink dress and been carried around on a chair. Asher moaned about Friday suppers but to me it sounded really nice. God and Asher's family seemed like a tight-knit bunch. When we went to church on Sundays, my father closed his eyes during the homily and took a little nap.

His family had something else mine didn't: a clarity, a cut-and-dried vision of who they were versus everyone else. We all left Europe after the war, his people and mine, but there was a subtle difference in what happened next. Asher had escaped something. Not all the Hungarians tried to get out; we even knew some Hungarians in Toronto who decided to go back. When my uncle outside Budapest proudly showed off his Czech-built Skoda, a car he'd spent seven years on a waiting list to own, even I knew that he was a participant in the system.

I told Asher how my mother and grandmother had crossed the forest in the middle of the night to escape Hungary before the Revolution—nothing like escaping the Nazis. He shook his head and agreed.

One day Asher and I were sitting in my grandmother's kitchen eating plum dumplings rolled in sugar. My grandfather was sitting in a big chair in the living room listening to Wagner. He was actually my step-grandfather; my real grandfather had been a maniac and my grandmother divorced him when she got to Canada.

My grandmother was standing by the stove. She nodded toward the living room, where her husband was relaxing with his eyes closed.

Without Wagner, she said, he would have been a dead duck!

She said he had been interviewed by a Wagner-loving SS officer in Vienna in 1938. What were the chances of an opera-loving Jew and an opera-loving Nazi falling into the same interview room together? My grandfather had a little notebook where he recorded every opera he'd ever seen; he and the SS agent had a really good talk. At the end of the interview, there was a loudspeaker announcement. Anyone holding a Polenpaß had to proceed to the train. *Polen* means Poland in German. A Polenpaß is a ticket to Auschwitz. The SS officer looked at my grandfather, who was holding his ticket. He handed him a second pass, a ticket for a boat to Shanghai.

My grandmother pulled two more dumplings out of the pot. When we were living in High Park, she said, he disappeared one night. She gestured to my grandfather with her spoon. Early in the morning I found him lying out on a park bench. He'd taken a lot of pills, you see.

His mother went to Auschwitz, my grandmother said. He never forgave himself.

She looked at Asher: They all have to try it once.

Where I went to school downtown, there were no other Hungarian girls at all and only two Hungarian boys, Gábor and Kálmán. Like all the full-grown Hungarian men I knew, their conversation started and stopped with opening a woman's legs.

I swore I'd never marry a Hungarian, my mother said as she arranged tomatoes and peppers on a plate for Sunday lunch.

My father of course was not just Hungarian; he was Transylvanian. This made him superior on many levels. The Transylvanians, he said, were the true Hungarians, Mongols left by Genghis Khan to colonize the Carpathian Mountains. These Mongol ancestors had left us with a language that bore no resemblance to those of our Slavic neighbours, an affinity for the training and riding of horses, and eyes so shallowly set that many of my aunts and uncles looked Asian—a fact I proudly pointed out to my friend My Le. My great-great-grandfather's likeness was embossed on the side of the biggest cathedral in Budapest. Strong as ten men, my father said, showing me a picture of the brass relief: a man in a rowboat, single-handedly saving the city from a flood.

I wanted to believe all these stories. The problem was that Hungary wouldn't cooperate. I didn't understand the politics but I knew that having money and buying things was good. When we went to Eastern Europe we had to line up at the border and bring used clothes for my cousins to wear. The biggest sin of communism was poverty.

At school I hid my ethnicity, sneaking the spicy salami out of my sandwich and eating plain rye bread and butter for lunch. When kids on the playground sang their own versions of popular songs—*I was Born in the USSR! So I moved to the USA!*—I felt implicated. We'd taken a trip back to Hungary the previous summer. In the small towns my relatives lived in identical, state-constructed apartment buildings and we walked from one aunt's house to the next, the old ladies lurching from side to side in their housedresses, gnarled feet in identical plastic sandals. On Saturday mornings they got up early to stand in line for bread and potatoes and sugar at the grocery store. We drove from village to village. When I got tired of looking at stork nests and sunflowers, I lay down in the back seat and listened to Bruce Springsteen and Laura Branigan on my Walkman.

In the country, things got a little more stark: Eat your soup! my mother hissed as I sat staring at dinner, a single chicken's claw groping out of a bowl of hot water.

When my grandmother's next student arrived, she put the rest of the dumplings on a piece of wax paper and Asher and I walked over to the plaza and back. It was only about two in the afternoon. Neither of us had any money and we sat around in the soft-carpeted basement of Asher's backsplit on Fairholme Avenue. Aside from all the regular basement stuff—television, card table folded against the wall, a few naugahyde chairs including a red La-Z-Boy out of which I had just flipped backward onto my head—there was a separate area that functioned as a storage space for the vending business. Little cartons of laundry soap and dryer sheets, plastic bottles of cheap perfume and stacks of packaged candy lined a crawl space that was only separated from the rec room by a low-slung saloon door.

Asher was sitting cross-legged in a beanbag chair. He flipped the remote. We were watching "When Doves Cry" on MuchMusic: Prince is in this steaming bathtub and then he gets up and you're supposed to think he's naked, but really he's got something around his waist that the camera wasn't meant to catch. MuchMusic was a brand new thing. There weren't any shows, just videos. Outside it was raining.

I am bored as shit, I said.

I looked over at the swinging saloon door and the stockpile of goods behind it. I always wanted to play store, or at least chew the gum and poke pinholes in the condoms, but Asher took his lower-management position to heart. He pulled a ledger out of the storeroom and tried to show me how he kept track of sales.

You're killing me, I said. I dropped off the La-Z-Boy onto the ground and lay there with my tongue hanging out sideways. I died. Your boringness made me die.

I'm not playing stupid House, Asher said. He was a little

irritated that his bookkeeping had failed to impress me.

I didn't say House! I sat up and leaned back on my hands. Who said House? Who was talking House?

We should play Escape, I said. We should play Houdini.

Asher looked thoughtful.

We can play Lock-Up, he said. He said he had some rope left over from an old Hallowe'en costume: maybe that would come in handy.

Yes! I said. Lock-Up!

At first we played with a stopwatch. We used the rope to tie the doors shut. Did Asher know, I wondered, that Houdini was Hungarian? I flexed my knuckles.

Big whoop, Asher said. I hate to break it to you, but you don't look anything like Houdini. You don't even look Hungarian, if you ask me.

He handed me the watch and went into the storage room. I laced the rope in and out between the hinges and then wrapped it around and around the doors, front to back. I wanted to secure the knots by stretching the rope out and tying it to the TV stand, but Asher protested. I can't reach all the way out there! he said. And what if I lurch the rope and the TV breaks?

I tied three knots and shook the doors with my hand to make sure they were tight together. We counted down from ten. When we got to "one," I pushed the button on the watch and Asher started trying to get out. My knots weren't all that good but they were on the outside of the doors so he had to reach his arms under and up to get to them. The real trick was figuring out how to hold your body to get maximum arm length under the doors. His first time through took him four minutes and three seconds. Then it was my turn. We counted down and I hit the deck, lying on my back and reaching up with my neck twisted a little and my shoulders right against the bottom of the doors. I made it out in three minutes twenty. We practiced back and forth like that. We found a little chalkboard in a corner of the storage room and used it to keep score. I beat Asher three times out of every four.

I have nimble fingers, I said, wiggling them in his face. He looked like he was losing interest so I let him win the next one, then came back for a final time of two-minutes-and-three.

Asher wiped out the chalkboard with his sleeve.

Hey! I said. I had been hoping to save my best score for the next time; it was pretty rare for me to be better than Asher at something. On our way upstairs I turned to him and suggested a rematch the following Saturday.

Nah, Asher said. We need to play it different next time. Like this, it's too easy.

I said that I hadn't noticed it being all that easy for him, but I was game to try something new.

One of us should be a guard, Asher said.

Like a jail, I said.

Like in a war, he said.

What I knew about war came from my own family. In the end pretty much everyone was on the German shit list. My father's uncle, the owner of a prodigious nose, was once asked to step into a Budapest alleyway and prove his heritage by unzipping his pants. Anyone with a foreskin was basically okay. He was Transylvanian nobility.

The village communists surrounded our house the night the Germans came in, my father said, nodding his head to any nonbelievers in the crowd. They wanted to protect us! My father's family resettled in the mountains over

Innsbruck. I'm sure they drove there in a car, but I liked to picture them hiking across a meadow wearing hats with little feathers like the von Trapp family in *The Sound of Music*. After they were gone, the Germans hung my father's uncle in effigy and put his furniture out in the rain. The village peasants used it in their living rooms if they had the space or in their farmyards if they didn't.

Like Hungary, Latvia was an Eastern Bloc country, but it was worse for two reasons: one, they were Slavs. I wasn't really sure what this meant, but the word sounded to me like the English *slaves* and so I knew that they had to be lower than Hungarians, who were horse-conquering Mongols. Two, Latvia was part of the USSR, which meant they were really Russians.

What I knew about Russia was that it had snatched Hungary up at the end of the war when Roosevelt was too busy being Stalin's friend to bother pushing him out. I knew what 60 Andrássy was: the four-story building in downtown Budapest where secret police interrogated anti-communists. On our last visit I'd gone shopping with my aunt Judit. We were walking west to the Oktogon metro station when she grabbed at my hand, pulling me along to make me go faster. I landed on both knees on the sidewalk, but my aunt didn't stop pulling. We were right in front of 60 Andrássy. Her father-in-law had spent two months there under interrogation in the 50s. It's a museum now, with a basement full of old torture devices, but in the 80s people were still afraid to walk by. My own great-grandfather had been sent to Siberia during the First World War.

His hands always shook a little, my father said, for the rest of his life. Like this: he held his hand out over the dinner table so that I could watch it tremble.

Okay, Asher said. War.

It was maybe two weeks later. The weather outside was still that kind of late spring rain that really hurts when it hits your face.

We got the saloon door all strung tight and the rope tied hard against the banister to upstairs, to the real house. We stood on the outside of the doorway admiring our handiwork.

If you were trapped in there, Asher said, no way could you get out. You couldn't get out unless someone took pity on you.

Those two ideas—*trapped* and *pity*—pushed up against one another in my mind. They were compelling to the imagination. They were caves and bears and jails and jailers all at the same time. Once when I was only three the girl across the street locked me in her garage and hung an old carpet over the door. I screamed and screamed to get out but nobody could hear me. I probably screamed for half an hour before my mother noticed I was missing and ran across the street in her apron and rubber gloves and opened the door.

You can be in Siberia, Asher said. You be a Hungarian villager and I'll be a Russian soldier and the lock-up is Siberia.

We can't do that, I said and Asher said How come? and I said because he really was Russian and I really was Hungarian and where was the fun in that. He rolled his eyes like I was making him play dolls or something when really this promised to be a very exciting game with trapping and escaping and who knew what else.

Fine, he said. He lowered his chin kind of. So you be the Jewish village girl and I'll be an SS and the lock-up can be a camp. The lock-up can be Bergen-Belsen, happy now?

I said, Yes. Now we were getting somewhere. Asher

got into character right away and pushed me into the storeroom and tied the rope tight. He twined the ends together and then made a final knot around the leg of an armchair, where I couldn't reach it. He didn't talk to me at all and I liked how fierce he made his mouth look.

I sat on my side of the saloon door and Asher sat out on the naugahyde chair. I could hear the noise of the television from upstairs where his mother was ironing and watching *Airwolf*. After a while I heard Asher's chair creak upright and he walked over to the door and peered at me through the hinges.

Don't chew the gum! he said.

I can't chew gum! I said. I'm a prisoner!

I really believed this. I was good at playing games. For a moment neither of us said anything. Upstairs, Asher's mother changed the channel to something with singing.

Now what? I said.

How should I know, Brainiac? Asher said. This is your stupid game.

War had been his suggestion. I didn't correct him. He was on his hands and knees on his side of the door, looking at me.

You should try to break out, he said.

What if I break the door?

I threw my hands up in the air like a hopeless person. You have to come in here, I said. You should come in here and order me around, or torture me or something. You have to torture me until I scream for mercy.

Asher shrugged, but he smiled a little, too. Torture as a notion was appealing enough for anyone our age and while he unpicked the knots I thought of all the stories my grandmother had forced on me while I was helping her to pull strudel dough nice and thin over the dining room table. How when the Russians came through they made the women kiss them, or they tied their knees together if they were trying to have babies. There were other stories, too: soldiers who fished around between your legs with a sword. When we'd been in Hungary, my teenaged cousin had made a gesture at me, a thing with his hands and his hips that I didn't understand, although I understood it to be unfriendly. I was lying in my aunt's room with my eyes mostly shut and he must have thought I was sleeping. For some reason that came to mind as well.

You have to tie my legs together, I said. You have to tie my legs and not untie them unless I kiss you. Asher set his jaw like he might say No, but then he didn't actually say anything.

I wanted to keep up the momentum. I had been watching *The Thornbirds* on television with my mother, at night when my father was out working. All that schmaltz. So I said, You have to make me kiss you like you're the last man on earth.

There was something deeply satisfying about this arrangement for both of us. Not so much the kissing part, although it was hard to resist. I liked feeling connected to an event. Here I was, an actual prisoner of war, about to escape or else not. Asher reeled in the rope from where it was hooked through the door. There was a lot of rope and he wrapped it around my legs about twenty times and then used the end of it to tie my wrists. I hadn't said anything about tying my wrists and I was glad to see him getting into the spirit of the thing. He took off his t-shirt and shoved it in my mouth. That really surprised me.

Pretend you're having a baby, he said.

I tried screaming into the t-shirt the way that women do on

TV but something about doing this actually sucks the breath right out of you. It was hard to get any air in through my nose, lying on the floor all tied up and with Asher kneeling next to me. His collarbone stood out under his shoulders and he had tiny pink nipples. He shoved my shoulder.

Come on, Asher said. Do something. Try and escape. Try it, try it, he said and he kept shoving at me. I was choking a little and I couldn't stop him pushing me because I was all tied up. We were both doing what we were supposed to do but the way he was pushing at me was the same way you kill a bug that you're a little afraid of. Where you need to get it into the Kleenex but it might jump on your hand and really scare you. He started yelling, You want me to untie you, you want me to untie you, pig? and I nodded my head and made some sounds into the t-shirt but then he changed it like we planned and said, I'll untie you but you have to kiss me, get it?

I didn't want to kiss him. I just wanted the t-shirt out of my mouth and I started shaking my head. I had tears in my eyes because I couldn't breathe and I could see Asher starting to panic because I wasn't playing along.

You have to say yes! Asher said. You have to say yes or I can't let you go!

I kept shaking my head and crying and Asher pushed his hands on my shoulders and my head banged off the hard ground and he started to cry too. He ripped the shirt out of my mouth.

His mouth was dry and mine was all wet from drooling into the shirt. I coughed against his lip. What the two mouths had in common was not wanting to be there, but we didn't know how else to end the game. If we'd just stopped it would have felt like hitting pause on a tape recorder. No matter what other game we played, the ending to Lock-Up would have hung over our heads like we'd stolen something and had to figure out how to put it back.

It was hard to stop crying. I was sucking at air in big gulps in a gaspy, sorrowful way. Jesus, Jesus, shut up! Asher said, working his fingers over the knot around my hands. My mother's going to hear you! Shut up, shut up!

I coughed a lot while he was untying me. Asher's mother called out: she wanted us to come upstairs and help her fold bedsheets. I turned back for a second on the way up. Asher's t-shirt was all wrinkled and spitty in the middle, where it had been bunched in my mouth, and he was trying to flatten it down against his chest. The whole upstairs was warm from the oven; his mother was baking something. I sat on the couch and folded the pillowcases into squares and stacked up the squares on the coffee table. Asher sat next to me. We didn't look at each other. I was afraid if I looked at his mother I'd start crying again. I didn't want to go back downstairs and I didn't want to go home either.

Asher's mother said, What you playing in the storeroom for? All that dust gonna kill you!

When it was dinner time Asher walked me back to my grandmother's. It was still raining so we had our hoods on. I kicked him once and then he shoved me and I said, Don't. We got in the wrong elevator by mistake. It was Shabbat. One of the elevators was pre-programmed to stop on every floor, so you don't have to press buttons on the sabbath. All the way to the fifteenth floor, the doors lurched open and closed.

Are you okay? Asher said.

I looked at myself in the mirrored walls.

This elevator sucks, I said. Oh no, I pushed a button!

God's going to kill me!

It was your stupid game, he said.

When I got inside I went into the bathroom and threw up in the toilet. I didn't know why I was sick.

I make you a cream-of-wheat! my grandmother called through the door.

The floor was cold and I sat there for a while with my hands on the white toilet seat. The whole room smelled like Oil of Olay. When I was little I used to go through the drawers and put on all the creams and draw pictures on my legs with the lipsticks, under my pants. The ends of the lipsticks got blunt and mashy and I hid them under a million tissues in the garbage. Once I stuffed my t-shirt with balled up Kleenex to see what I would look like with breasts; when I tried to flush the tissues, the toilet overflowed and I lied and said I'd used the Kleenex to mop the floor.

Asher was waiting around for me to come out but I wanted just nothing, I wanted him to yell Goodbye! through the door so that I could be alone in the bathroom, maybe forever. I heard him tell my grandmother about the elevator. I think she's sea-sick, he said.

Down near the base of the toilet there were some yellow stains. I could smell the cream-of-wheat boiling in the kitchen. My throat was harsh from crying and then vomiting. My grandmother's icon of Mary sat there on top of it all: her body held open and her red heart all lit up like an eye.

ACCIDENTAL PONDS

The weather was humid and this made the hostel door stick.
I threw my weight against it and fell into the room. Your
pink sandals and your pack were lying in a corner. You were
there too, asleep, face turned toward the window. I had to
walk around in my socks so as not to wake you, run the tap
on low when I washed my hands. I had come into Rennes
earlier in the evening and dropped my bag on an empty bed.
There were two keys to the room; I saw that one of them was
already taken. Out walking, I measured my steps along a set
of canals. It was already dark. I didn't have a map.

I sat in a bar on the main street and wrote letters. A
dark green awning stretched over the sidewalk but inside
the place felt more like a club than a brasserie. Dark wood
floor, small tables, no booths. I had left both a boyfriend
and another man more than twice my age. I'd left them
behind and flown to France, planning to stay for months,
but I couldn't stop writing to them. A couple in their 40s sat
at the next table beneath a print of one of Dufy's bullfights
and watched me write. He was drinking cognac. She had
that French hair: black, cut straight. The scrape of her chair
along the floor as she moved closer and tucked a strand of

my own hair behind my ear. This seemed entirely natural. Where are you from, the man wanted to know. Where are you staying. Is there any place we can drive you. When I left the bar I kept checking over my shoulder. It was after midnight and I walked in the middle of the road, beside the parked cars. Someone had left their bicycle chained to a fence and it was missing both its wheels. I learned that there was more than one set of canals.

I stopped at a gas station to ask directions. The attendant couldn't let me in because the door was set on automatic lock. He slid open a small window and pushed a hand-drawn map at me. A taxi will take too long to get here, he said. You need to get home quickly.

At the hostel I rang the bell and waited for a boy with a red mohawk and a dog to let me in.

In the morning you painted your toes with clear polish: a few bristles fell off the brush and stuck to your nails. You already had a plan with a boy named Nigel. He was driving a car he'd bought from relatives in Holland. He can go places the trains won't take us, you said. The Bretons believe this was Arthur's kingdom. You invited me along to see Merlin's tomb and Morgaine's lake.

In the room both of us tried to take a shower. There was a drain, but the floor didn't even slant. The water spread out like fingers. We stood on the beds and screamed, and hauled our things, bags and shoes, up onto the covers. We had to jump for the door when we wanted to leave.

You brought me down to the street where Nigel was waiting. He saw me with you and pretended to be glad. The car had only three gears: we drove 80 kilometres an hour all through Bretagne and everybody on the road hated us. You were from England and he was from Australia. We were like a reunion of colonies in a slow, slow car. I told you how my godmother had warned me against coming to Rennes. She said it was ugly, but I told you it reminded me of Canada. It was the first French place I'd been where I could see a connection to home.

The three of us stayed in an old farmhouse they'd turned into a hostel. The rooms were like dormitories. The women's room had rows of beds on two sides, set under the dormers. It made me think of an old musical my mother liked to watch, about seven girls trapped in a house with seven brothers. When we slept in those beds, we were like those girls. We bought bread and cheese in the village. Nigel had food we hadn't seen in France: peanut butter, vegemite. We were starved for peanut butter. There was no kitchen and we ate off plastic bags on a picnic table in the yard, cutting everything with the same knife.

We rented bicycles. We biked down between the trees on small roads and the ferns came to our shoulders. I was out in front, used to hills, you and Nigel behind. I had to stop pedalling and coast so as not to lose you. Nigel was surprised that my legs were so strong. It embarrassed him.

Once a week I called my boyfriend in Canada and cried into the phone. I missed him in a practiced way, full of guilt and habit. We'd been living together a year. But I knew if I went home I would betray him again. The other man was a fifty-minute streetcar ride from my apartment. In the beginning I didn't even know why I was making the trip. I would just dance up and down on one side of his kitchen counter and drink a lot of coffee. One day I sat on the arm of his couch, telling him things, and he stood behind me and slid his hands down into the neckline of my shirt. The tips of his fingers against my nipples. This is something I allowed. Once I brought over a book of poetry I loved and he said, about the author, She used to live here for a while. They'd been married while I was still in nursery school.

He was someone I met on a job interview. I was about to graduate and thinking very keenly about what I might do with my life. On the way home from the interview I did what Mary used to do in the opening credits of *The Mary Tyler Moore Show*, where she threw her hat up in the air and spun around. It was April, but still quite cold.

The first time I saw him, we went to see a documentary about a woman who ran a brothel. I called my boyfriend and said I was staying downtown with this other man. It wasn't a secret; everyone knew we were friends. My boyfriend said nothing to me about this friendship. We never fought about it. We were both pretending I was someone I'm not. I don't know how to explain this. It was like walking a worn path: you just can't see anything else, or any other way. Other people were more suspicious. They asked, What does a forty-five-year-old man want with a twenty-two-year-old girl?

You can say this the other way around: What does a twenty-two-year-old girl want with a forty-five-year-old man. One day we were in bed and I looked down and saw a bra lying on the floor. Lace. C cup. He told me there was a woman living in his house. She'd been living there a year; they were trying to have a baby. The woman had once had a baby with someone else, but that baby died.

You told me you were sleeping with your professor. He had invited you to live in his house in Manchester, with him and his wife. One night he came upstairs. I'm in my nightgown, you said, and he sits down on the edge of my bed and I start to cry.

You had a boyfriend, too, with whom you were trying to work things out. We looked upon this coincidence like a lost ring found in the pocket of a coat you haven't worn for a year.

Everything was a mess, and we walked enormous distances together. We walked instead of hitchhiking. I wanted to see the house of Mme. de Sévigné. You said, There is no hostel in Vitré. We found a room in the tiny Hôtel de la Gare across from the station and couldn't believe the luxury. You flung yourself onto your bed and said, Brilliant. Feathers. In the mornings you ordered the breakfast with tea while I took coffee, so that we could both have tea and then coffee. I still do that. I did it today.

It was a long walk to Les Rochers, where Sévigné lived. She was a widow at twenty-six and never remarried. She knew her letters were being circulated immediately and managed to write for both a private and a public eye. She got away with quite a lot and I wanted to know how she had done it.

In the mornings I crouched over the toilet and vomited. The smell of tobacco: men smoking on the sidewalk before work. You guessed before I told you, smoothed the hair from my face. I ate very little and my belly stayed flat. I taught you all the words to the best Janis Joplin songs as we walked. When it poured we tied kerchiefs on our heads until they soaked through. The sun shone through the rain. I said, When that happens, it means the devil is beating his wife.

A month later, I stopped throwing up. Holed up in my godmother's Paris studio on Avenue Kléber. Three days of cramps, the soft lining of my body tearing itself apart, then finally a bony clot, purple in the toilet bowl. When it was done I planned a hiking trip: Tuscany, or Ireland, places I'd meant to go before going home. Somewhere the villages were spaced a day's walk apart.

Instead I got into bed. I slept, or lay there with my eyes closed, on three pillows, the covers drawn up over my hair. I was cold all the time. I couldn't get warm. I had dreams that I was awake but couldn't move. In the dreams I saw my own legs and feet stretched out near the end of the bed, my arms loose across my stomach. I tried to lift the arms, to slap myself awake, or throw my legs off the side onto the floor. Just as I sat up, the tape looped and I had to start over again. All of this long after you left.

I have photographs of us, the ones you sent after we'd both gone home. They arrived in their blue envelope from Boots Drugstore, and were so large and glossy compared to my pictures. I wondered if this was your choice, or if that's just how photographs look in England. You, sitting on a wall, the Lady of the Lake. Me in a monk's garden, squinting into the sun and wearing a pair of shorts, cut off high. Tidy rows of vegetables on either side. Sitting out at night in Rennes, a fountain streaming behind us, the lights blurring past as if we were spinning. As if we were moving so fast the camera couldn't catch us.

Drunk on cider. Teenaged boys walking by us in packs, yelling out to one another. Sitting out front of the striped houses. I'm learning to mimic the way you talk, using old words in new ways. Knickers. Brilliant. Nice, meaning good-looking. Rhyming things up, linen draper for newspaper. China plate for best mate. At home in Canada, my next boyfriend will ask me to say the word *can't* over and over again. Can't, can't. I can't.

It takes a long time to pull you from my mouth.

That was some nice guy, at the end there.

I'm twisting an earring, round and round. It's a new one, and still stings a little when I move it. Tossing about my new vocabulary.

I don't know. I was looking at you.

There is a long moment as we consider this. We've been sitting cross-legged on our feathery beds, facing each other. Like girls at camp. Sleeping in our t-shirts.

You wanted to walk with your eyes closed and asked me to lead you. We were somewhere between Vitré and Fougères. Hiking through fields. It was just beginning to rain. The drops were undefined, somehow our faces were getting wet. Your mouth slightly open as you walked. Delighted. Fingers twisted against mine.

I thought you would sink your foot into a hole and collapse. I didn't want to be responsible for this. Some of the fields were flooded. The ground was sponge beneath our shoes. There were accidental ponds with animals in them, ducks, a big mallard beating on a white farm duck, pushing its head under the water. I'd never seen anything like it and couldn't move. It scared you. You grabbed at my wrists, my elbows. You had to pull me by the hand and drag me away.

We were apart for a few days. I had promised to meet a friend of a friend, a Master's student in philosophy, at Mont Saint-Michel. When I got there the hostel provided only plastic-covered mattresses. I lied and said I'd brought my own bedsheets: they didn't allow anyone to stay without blankets. I slept in all my clothes, layers of shirts and pants. By eleven in the morning the tourists were so thick I couldn't breathe.

The Master's student only wanted to get drunk. He asked me if I'd ever cheated on my boyfriend.

I wrote to you once, months later. Do you remember that? I wanted to let you know how everything turned out. In the letter I told you how I almost reached out to you that night. How close that was for me, the closest I've ever been. When you wrote back, you were ecstatic. You had moved in with your boyfriend. He liked to bring you croissants at work, at eleven o'clock. He made you tea, then coffee in the mornings. You left some code for me at the end of the letter: *p.s.*, you wrote. *About what you said. I know what you mean.*

We took the train into Grenoble. This meant the night before we had to sleep on the station floor in Lyon. It was a morning train. We'd been half the night dancing and didn't want to spend the money on a hostel. There was no one else waiting. There are no night trains in Lyon.

Two conductors on their way home scuffed their shoes against the floor nearby. Where are you going, one of them asked. They were still wearing their SNCF caps and the little pins they have on their jackets, the French flag. Before I could stop you, you said, Grenoble. He pointed to the next platform. That's the train right there, he said. Why don't you get on and sleep there instead? This floor's too dirty.

You imagined this to be a gesture of kindness or generosity and I followed you even though I knew better. It wasn't my first trip to France.

When they climbed aboard behind us you were shocked. I said, Grab your bag. I had to say it three times. I knew it was possible for them to lock the doors. It was a long walk down to the end of the car and we threw our bags ahead of us and jumped off onto the platform. We left the station and drank café au lait in an all-night *bar-tabac*, at a table on the sidewalk. Did you know? you asked me. Did you know that would happen?

I said, I thought you understood what you were getting into.

The last time I saw you we were just north of Avignon. Your family had a connection there, a fat man who lived in a town carved out of a cliff. You wanted me there so you would be safe in his house. He was going to dinner with friends and asked us to come. We took his key instead, walked through a church garden, drank cocktails outdoors at the very highest point in the town. We wore shoes we liked and got blisters walking up the hill to get there. We drank French cocktails: Campari-orange, Pernod. At night we slipped home. Inside, there were two sets of stairs, one to his and one to our side of the house. We climbed up to our room and slept in the same bed, legs touching.

FIELD WORK

We wanted to learn about the men. The old stories had all been forgotten. A study was commissioned. Our lead investigator stretched a hand up against the chalkboard, high over her head. Men were once as tall as women, she told us. Taller.

When had the men shrunk? we asked, but she couldn't say. At some point they had become tiny, the length of your hand. That much we knew.

We went into the wild to find them. Together we were a world-class team. This project, we told each other, was no different from our other field experience, studying the black rhino or the digger wasp. Our best and brightest associate professors took to the task of grant-writing, myself among them. The funding rolled in and we rolled up our sleeves.

Shifts were divided. Equipped with field glasses and collapsible chairs, we constructed blinds so as not to be noticed. Even in densely populated areas, the men lived alone. At regular intervals they emerged from their homes—caves or small holes in the ground—in order to forage. Some team members observed the men while they were awake and active. We installed tiny cameras and watched them while they slept.

After six months I said aloud what many of us had been thinking.

The men are not providing us with enough information! I banged my cup on the dining hall table. How do they grow? What do they want?

I aligned myself with another researcher. We held meetings after hours and made lists and lists of questions. In partnership, we created a new study that would follow the men from their formative, pre-man years. This was to be our life's work. My partner took charge of the Centre for Specimen Generation. It was her job to sweep the men's holes for tissue, sample the tissue for DNA, fill our test tubes with nutritive agar. We built glass enclosures, fifteen per lab, and incubated the bodies as if they were our own babies. Sturdy volunteers pushed the tiny pre-men out from between their legs.

Predictably, we divided into factions. My research team argued for an increasingly close relationship with the men. Authenticity, we said, depends on empathy. We held a naming ceremony, carried their photos in our wallets.

Some believed the intimacy of this process compromised the study as a whole. These dissenters were removed from the project.

Are we field researchers? the outgoing Chair screamed, and she watched as the Maid Brigade cleaned out her desk—their blue uniforms, their embroidered name tags. I straightened my white coat and stood firm. The lab, I told my loyal colleagues, can be whatever you want it to be. The lab can be the field.

• • •

In infancy, the pre-men were voracious. They required constant nourishment and lapped up whatever we squeezed into their open mouths. We were delighted. This greed was marvelous and worth recording. We hunched over the enclosures, sharpened our pencils, adjusted our magnifiers. When a blonde graduate student whispered, They are just like regular babies!, I took a stern tone and waited until she gathered herself.

The pre-men gurgled into the drone of the lab's fluorescent light.

All science, I said to the room, is the search for unity in hidden likeness, and the blonde student copied this into her notebook, underlining vigorously.

Next the pre-men grew mobile. They went from lying still to kicking out with all four limbs. When one was observed trying to escape by slinking backwards along the floor, using his feet and shoulders to push his body along, we applauded. I picked him up with a pair of tongs dedicated to this purpose and replaced him in the enclosure.

The success of these early observations advanced exponentially, as did our pride. Our articles were published in the most prestigious journals. Conferences were organized, awards were conferred, meals were elaborately catered.

We gave each other high fives. We were learning about the men.

As they began to stand erect, the pre-men became harder to keep track of. They flexed their tiny biceps and coalesced into groups. They enjoyed toys with wheels. In a report to the Dean of Sciences, I wrote: As a species, the men are found to be both social and aggressive. She agreed that as the pre-men grew we would isolate them in increasing degrees.

At the thirteen-year mark, the pre-men became hairy. They formed circles and pummeled each other with tiny fists, flattening each other's noses. My research partner, by this time my chief colleague in the Bureau of Pre-Man Observation, wrote paper after paper exploring the possible reasons for this behaviour. Were these circles Druidic in nature? The nose-flattening—could this be some kind of ritual marker? Did they need to bleed as they entered adolescence in an effort to align themselves with women?

We made them clothes. Their moving parts had begun to move too frequently. At times they moved close to one another. Are they lonely? my partner asked me. Sometimes they look at me with such eyes.

It was her idea that tiny women be generated. I think they like us, she said at the first board meeting of the month. I think if there were tiny women, they would fight less.

The pre-men require a physical outlet, I said. Give them some rocks to push around.

We gave them rocks and they threw them at each other.

Whoops, I said. Larger rocks. The pre-men pushed the larger rocks around and pummeled each other all the same.

The others had questions: How often were they turning to one another? What exactly had my partner seen, and at what time of day?

At a later meeting I asked how she proposed to create tiny women. She regarded me from her side of the room, but her hands only rose and fell at her sides. I pushed my chair back from the table.

They will fight less in isolation, I said.

I said, We are the only women here.

•••

We reconstructed the small homes we had observed years before in the wild, burrows dug into the ground. The pre-men entered and exited these burrows. I was first to initiate a locality study. Do you see how each man takes his bearings upon leaving the den? I asked, and at that moment a brown-haired man poked his torso from the entrance to his cave. It was as though he could understand my language, as though he wanted for me what I wanted for myself. How unknowable my descending hand must have seemed to him! How like weather! How like his creator! We had a short and unequal struggle. I pinned his shoulders to the earth and used a bottle of nail enamel (Second-Hand Rose) to tag the back of his neck. Then I let him go.

After only two weeks of this procedural, observers reported that, at any one time, ten men, each marked by colour (Matte Mardi Gras, Purrfect Purrple, the original subject in Second-Hand Rose), were within view. We were encouraged to see that the tagged men found their way back to their own dens in a consistent fashion. The simple trick of marking the men had changed our attitude toward them. Tracking and recording their movements created in us a feeling of pride of ownership. Their lives became of invested concern. It was decided that each of us would be assigned a particular subject. I stood up first and claimed my brown-haired specimen and the others nodded their assent.

I now suggested that we alter the routes into and away from the dens. With the men held safely at an alternate facility, we relocated all distinguishing markers: twigs, pebbles, anything found lying around inside the enclosures. We used trowels to alter the landscape. The dens themselves were left intact. We waited to observe the men's return.

Their behaviour was striking. They appeared confused

and wandered in circles. We repeated the test and recorded the same result every time. By moving landmarks, we could do more than disorient the men. We controlled their movements. We made them go to entirely different dens.

Observational distance allowed us to extend our research in new directions. When we covered their eyes with black paint (Goin' Jet), the men were unable to navigate and stayed in their dens, alone.

•••

There is now little doubt that our locality studies widened the field for an entirely new generation of behavioural scientists. Despite this proven success, years later a group of scientists—led by my former partner—would begin to probe the conventions of our methods. They took issue with the subject-researcher relationship. Power-structured, they called it. Unusually manipulative. It was a rift.

What my colleague is suggesting, I wrote in an open letter to *XX* magazine, is insulting. Nothing less than a call for chaperones. Why, after all this time, should I submit to another scientist looking over my shoulder? Despite my protests, funds were diverted toward the formation of a Bio-Ethical Standards Caucus, a branch devoted to the study of why the outcomes of our tests delighted us so. At the next All Fields Conference, I asserted that the objectivity of these researchers was now compromised.

You are wasting our time and you are wasting our money, I said. As to the specimens, are we subjecting them to illness? What injections are you protesting? What injuries?

They lead bloody happy lives, I said. Redirect your efforts to other fields.

My former partner stood up. She needed assistance and leaned heavily on the shoulder of her post-doctoral student, a red-haired woman with shapeless, solid ankles. My partner's thin wrist shook.

This study has been the focus of my entire professional life, she said. You can't kick me out for disagreeing with your methods.

I offered incentives to the red-haired doctoral candidate, and she stood to cross the room. When her student removed the shoulder, my colleague fell.

The men, too, had grown older. Their hair had begun to gray, their movements came slower. They spent less and less time pushing the rocks. After the conference, I returned to the lab and washed my hands. I stood over my brown-haired subject's enclosure. I pushed at his stomach, his chest. He reached out suddenly and grasped my finger, pulling the whole weight of his body into my hand.

We, I said. His tiny blacked-out eyes turned toward my voice. Using a cotton swab, I removed the paint from his eyes. For the first time in years, he could see. He blinked.

I bent closer, thinking of his eye reflected in mine. My eye an enormous speckled mirror.

When my former partner died at ninety-two, we draped her stiff frame in the university flag and lowered her into the ground, into a hole that had been filled with rose petals. There was a violinist: she had admired Berlioz. A minister, not I, gave the eulogy. Afterward we had the usual coffee and sandwiches in the boardroom. Crustless, on white or rye or brown. Egg or salmon or ham and mayonnaise, with cream for the coffee in lidded pitchers.

What was left of my partner's faction returned to older studies, field work that had not drawn attention for a generation: evidence for the extinction of a Lowland Gorilla species, or of the Cape Goose. Younger researchers began studies of their own and turned up their noses at our affiliations. Those who stayed on with me demanded soft chairs.

We are brittle, they said, from years of standing over our enclosures.

At an average age of seventy-three-point-eight years, the men began to expire. We had generated so many of them all at once. They died and died.

We looked at each other.

The tiny bodies stacked up in piles.

HE ATE HIS FRENCH FRIES IN A LIGHT-HEARTED WAY

On my nineteenth birthday I went out for a beer with this guy Jamie Nash. I didn't want to go. I'd been getting into bars since I was fifteen, the age-of-majority hoopla was lost on me. But Jamie called up and made such a fuss. Tradition! he said. I ended up feeling like I owed him one.

We split a pitcher in a place close to where my parents live. Sports on the television. Not boxing, which I like to watch when I'm just sitting in a bar. I was home from university for Thanksgiving weekend. It was my first year. Some people get home and run around like crazy trying to see everyone they know, but all I had done so far was sleep. I slept thirteen hours a night three nights in a row, numbers that shocked me. I went to bed at a regular time and when I woke up it was afternoon. There were voices right outside my window. I opened the curtains and kids on bikes were yelling at each other. Cats were just walking up and down the street because all the cars were at work. I've always been someone who gets by on very little sleep. I'd only been away for a couple of months but I felt disconnected. It didn't surprise me to be sitting in a crummy sports bar on my birthday.

Jamie had his camera with him and he took some pictures of me across the table, the usual weird stuff: my knuckles, part of my collarbone. I leaned my head and shoulder against the steamed-up window next to my chair. When I sat up again my hair was wet. The jukebox was right behind where Jamie was sitting and every time the song changed he drummed the table, then leaned back and read off the name. This is Thelma Houston, he said. Now it's Uriah Heep. He kept switching our glasses so I wouldn't know whose was whose.

I told him about a place I liked to go when I was away at school. They make their own brew, I said. And they have half-price burgers if you order before six. All the chairs are armchairs and they're made of leather, so you bring all your reading with you and you curl up and this girl Season I'm friends with always falls asleep.

Her name is Season?

And there's a dance club called Autowerk, only the mosh pit gets totally intense, you can get hurt super easy.

I had one leg crossed over the other and the dangling foot was bouncing up and down. I looked down and watched the foot.

In September I picked up this guy by just crashing into him over and over again, I said. Then finally he decided I was pretty cute and he should take me home.

Jamie unscrewed the camera lens, zipped it into its case, and put the whole thing under his chair. He cupped his hand around my elbow, which made me spill my beer a little.

What are you doing, I said.

Jamie said, Have you heard anything about Del?

My friend Del had been pretty sick before I left in September. I'd sent him a letter via Jamie.

I don't know, I said. I wrote to him, but he never wrote me back. Did you give him the letter?

I thought maybe you'd call him, Jamie said. After the letter, I mean. I gave it to him. I mean like follow-up.

I got up to go to the bathroom and when I came back, there was another full pitcher. Are you kidding me? I said. I want to go to bed. Jamie grinned at me very wide.

Yeah, me too, he said.

There was something on the top of my shoe. It was Jamie's foot, kicking at me under the table. He was having a really good time.

On the way home he tried to kiss me in the school playground, standing up on the log fence. It had been raining and the top of each log was slick with October frost. When I saw Jamie's open mouth coming at me I wasn't surprised. It was slippery, but I'm a master of the head-turn. We'd been friends for a long time.

Back in high school I worked at a bookstore that specialized in rare and pricey things. That was upstairs, where my friend Del sat behind a big desk. Del had black muttonchop sideburns and loved science fiction. I don't want to tell you what kinds of authors he liked, because I can never remember the difference between the good science fiction and the bad stuff and I might make a mistake and say the wrong name. That would feel like libel. Downstairs, where I worked, were all the regular books: self-help and business and a wall of popular fiction. There was a guy in a grey suit who liked to wait around outside the door until whoever else I was working with stepped out for a coffee. Then he'd slink in and ask for recommendations. Have you read this one? he'd say, and hold up the Marquis de Sade or Anaïs

Nin or whatever else he could find lying around. I was sixteen when I started working there. He wore the kind of tie that has little golf clubs on it. Or sometimes bull terriers.

I was the only kid at that store. The owners didn't want teenagers. Del was thirty when I met him. The first day we worked together, I was sitting down behind the counter and he came up behind me and started massaging my shoulders. He pressed his thumbs into the hard spots. First I thought, Here we go again. But then I thought about Marguerite Duras and how I could learn a lot from an older man, and my shoulders really stiffened up.

Del said, Relax, honey, I'm not a perv. I'm just an old fag. He wore a wedding band, which wasn't common in those days.

We used to go to dinner all the time, but the sicker he got, the less he could eat. We went to Ginza and he sat in the restaurant and let his bowl of soba noodles go cold. It was my last year of high school. We'd known each other for a couple of years. I just talked and talked so we could both pretend not to notice how much he wasn't eating. I'm going to borrow my mother's car on Sunday, I said. Isn't this wallpaper nice?

Del's boyfriend was a hairdresser who worked out of their kitchen on Church Street. We came in after dinner one night with bottles of mix for margaritas and Jeff was standing over a TV host I recognized, clipping away. Skinny lines of coke on the Formica tabletop. I asked Del if he minded the coke. He said No. He can do what he wants with his nose, is what he said. Del's problems had started after Jeff hooked up with some other guy at a rave, but Jeff wasn't sick. Just Del was.

I once smoked a joint that was laced with crack, I said.

How was that? Del said. I didn't know if he meant, how did that happen, or how was the high.

The same I guess, I said. I didn't really notice. Someone told me later. We were at a party, I probably only had a couple puffs.

Nah, don't lie to me, Del said. You're a coke queen. You know it.

We sat in Del's bedroom until the kitchen turned back into a kitchen again. We had the blender with us and Del was chipping frozen lime mix out of the cardboard tube with a spoon. It was scooping out in tiny chunks, chink chink, against the blades in the bottom of the blender.

Del said, What am I doing? I'll just throw it up anyway.

We thought we'd try the margaritas for fun. At least you'll be drunk, I told him. Those were the days before they gave you free pot just because you had AIDS.

After Jamie tried to kiss me in the schoolyard, we walked home like nothing had happened. I went inside and he got on the bus and that was it. I watched some TV and ate a piece of cornbread. Jamie's family lived in a very big old house near High Park, and he did bizarre things. Like if you went over to his house he might make you a pear omelette. He was probably my best friend from high school. He had a hookah that Del sold him after a trip to Morocco, and sometimes we'd cook a little hash in it and pretend it was opium.

Hanging around Del always made me feel like I was very sophisticated about drugs, but mostly I smoked a little grass between classes and that was it. At my high school, rolling was a very gender-specific activity. I'm still not much good. It's one of my biggest regrets. So a guy could pass you anything rolled into a joint and you would smoke it. My friend Larissa claimed that she'd had the best sex of her life after we smoked that crack. I was on the ceiling, she said. And I could see my body down on the floor. I was looking all around the room.

Maybe you should have kept looking down, I said. What was your body doing that was so good? But Larissa said her body was the same; it was the crack that made the difference. I was pretty sure her boyfriend had made the crack story up. Who did they even buy it from? They had a hard enough time getting decent grass.

The boyfriend's name was Bill. He and Larissa spent a lot of time fighting. Bill had a car and he liked to drive to other cities and party with other girls. That was a sticking point. I dragged Jamie around with me wherever I went, which gave me some protection against losers because most people weren't sure if we were a couple or not. Every now and then he'd go to hold my hand or rub his cheek against my neck or something and I'd have to say, Slow down, Chaka Khan. We're pretending, remember?

I decided that I'd better call him and make sure he got home all right. The phone had to ring nine times before anyone even picked it up.

It's two in the morning, Jamie said. You woke up my Mom.

Oh, I said, I'm not really used to people living at home anymore.

Jamie didn't say anything to that. I thought of something else.

I guess I just wanted to make sure you're okay.

Okay, like how?

Just okay, I said. Like, you know.

Like how, Jamie said. Is there something you want to talk about?

I switched the phone to my other ear.

Okay, like you totally put the moves on me again and I denied you. Okay, like that. I waited for him to answer. There were some crumbs from the cornbread stuck under my fingernails and I fiddled them out.

Yeah, Jamie said. That's whatever.

I just don't want there to be misunderstandings, I said. I mean, I think you were just drunk and these things happen. I told him about Abraham Maslow's hierarchy of needs, and how after food and shelter, sex was the very most important thing. So it's not really your fault, I said. Your drunk brain is just doing what it thinks it should.

Holy, Jamie said. You're a real piece of work, you know that?

He said, It's totally fine. You don't want to get laid, that's totally fine with me. I have another girlfriend anyway. I have six other girlfriends.

You don't have six other girlfriends.

In fact, I do.

Anyway, I said. I was never your girlfriend, Jamie. You get that, right?

Yes, he said. I get that. Can I go to bed now?

One of us hung up, but I don't remember who.

I used to bring boys I liked into the store so Del could tell me which ones were worth my time. I mean, before he got too sick to work. He always liked the ones I only wanted to be friends with, which annoyed me. I knew a guy that rode a motorbike, but he was the wrong kind of guy with a bike. He was very compact and cheerful and the bike was a Suzuki. Del loved him. His name was Brett Furnival, he used to pick me up at night and we'd go riding through the bike trails along the Don River. There were no lights at all except the light on the bike. At the entrance to the trail was a big sign with a picture of a motorcycle crossed out: No Motorized Vehicles. I waited for Brett to say something about how we weren't supposed to do this, but all he said was, This is really fun! Are you holding on?

We never got caught and we never hit a tree. Brett would never have taken any chances on a ride like that.

Someone else that Del loved was Jamie Nash. I suspected that Del was coaching him. On my last birthday Jamie had come into the store and bought me these whopping big art books, hardcovers I could never afford because I spent all my money on other things. *Daumier to Picasso: The Pleasures of Paris* and *Karsh: A Sixty Year Retrospective.* I was stuck behind the cash and Jamie and Del were hidden in the stacks, talking loud and dropping things. I stuck out my tongue at them, but then an old lady wanted to talk to me about dictionaries.

Jamie didn't give me the books until we were at his house. We were going to hang out and watch *Belle de Jour*, because I liked to pretend I was French. It was a movie I had picked, and Jamie didn't like it. This is stupid, he said. And you've seen this before? Why would you sit through this twice? We were lying around in his room watching the movie, and I was arguing with him because there was nothing wrong with it. At the end of the night, he put my car keys down his pants. You've got to be fucking kidding me, I said. Are you serious? Seriously, this is what we're doing now?

Jamie said, Come and get them.

We hadn't even been drinking.

I stood up on the bed.

You can't go home, Jamie said. I've got your keys.

You know what? I said. I don't want my keys.

What I wanted to do was be very hard-assed and silent, with just my open, waiting hand to make him feel guilty. But instead of that I started yelling.

Fucking take them out of your pants and wash them! I said. I'm going home! I jumped up and down with both feet on the mattress. Jamie was on the ground in front of me, which made him shorter than usual. He ran backwards and forwards like he was a football player doing warm-up exercises. Come and get them! Come and get them! he kept saying. I was waving my arms like a crazy person and stomping his pillows. I wanted something dramatic and feathery to occur, but the pillows were Polyfill, so I had to be happy just making them flat.

Eventually Jamie gave up and handed me the keys and I backed down the driveway doing sixty. The squealing tires made it sound like I was still yelling.

I only ever had one boyfriend in high school, and it wasn't Jamie Nash. His name was Max Shapiro. It lasted about six weeks. Del used to call him Ponyboy, and asked me not to bring him into the store.

Max was like the captain of the football team for stoners. Everybody knew him. He had long black hair in a braid down his back and a brown suede jacket with fringe along the shoulders. He was twenty-one in grade thirteen. Everywhere he went, he said things like, Hey cat, got any bread?

People couldn't get enough of him.

Max was one of those guys that will do anything to get high, just anything. I once watched him carve a water pipe out of a little kid's bath toy. Another time, at a party, he and his friends sat around in a circle eating chunks of raw nutmeg.

What are you doing? I said. The nutmeg looked really chewy and they were forcing it down with lots of water.

Max said, You can totally get high off nutmeg.

They looked pretty pleased with themselves. For about five minutes. Then the vomiting began. The guy whose house it was ran around in circles trying to get them all to stop throwing up on his Mom's carpet. He had a roll of paper towel and he kept throwing sheets of it toward the floor so he wouldn't have to get too close. Jeez! he yelled. Jeez!

I never had a lot of luck getting high school boys to ask me out, so I really liked being Max's girlfriend. In grade eleven a boy named Spilios Roumeitis tutored me in algebra for free. That was the closest I got. We met in the school basement early in the morning and I sat on the concrete floor with the textbook open on my stretched-out legs. Or he'd pass me his notes in English class. The math wasn't too hard, as it turned out. The last thing I heard, Spilios Roumeitis had a lacrosse scholarship to the University of Michigan and was studying to become a neurosurgeon, so probably I should have acted dumber or giggled more or something. I don't know.

With Max, other girls would come up to me when I was trying to have a quiet smoke behind the athletics hut and say, Are you really going out with Max Shapiro? And if they meant, was I having terrible sex with him in other people's basements, then yes sir, I was dating him. One time we were all over at Larissa's house, baking potatoes in the fireplace and playing strip poker. Part of the trick with this game, if you were a girl, was that they never really wanted to teach you the rules of poker, so we had crafted a bylaw whereby if you were down to your underwear you could opt to do some jumping jacks instead of taking off your bra. Larissa's brother came home and said, I missed the jumping jacks again? He was fifteen.

Max was usually pretty sharp with the cards but this time things weren't going so well for him. He went into the bathroom for a long time. When he came out he played a bad hand. Don't ask me what it was, I don't know anything about poker. He took off his boxers and started streaking around the room but there was something pink stuck to him. Is he wearing Lycra? I said. Oh my God, Larissa said. That's my mother's girdle. I came from a house where no one ever wore a girdle, so I didn't know what the pink thing was.

At the end of the six weeks we had an enormous fight at a party. Max lay on his stomach on someone's mother's bed and said, Betrayed, betrayed. At the end of the night he got up and I shoved him down the hall. Then I drove home drunk and high as a kite and in the morning I had to get up and look out the window to check that the car was really in the driveway.

After I dated Max, I didn't see Jamie as much. It became something we had to work at. Before that, being friends had been an easy thing. We hung around together in an accidental sort of way, out in the alley or drinking coffee down the street when I was supposed to be in German class. He'd come by the store and hang around for almost a whole evening shift, showing Del his photographs and bugging me. I didn't care so much whether or not Jamie came and saw me, but Del started looking thinner and needing to sit down more, and I thought me and Jamie joking around all evening would really cheer him up. I left Jamie voicemail messages. You never come over, I said.

I was on my own for the weekend because my parents were visiting people who had a cottage. A friend of my

Dad's was supposed to be checking in on me at night. Since I had the house to myself, I decided to learn how to wax my bikini line. There was the pot of wax, goopy and hot on the stove. The whole place smelled like the kind of candles you buy at the health food store. I was upstairs in the bathroom listening to Iggy Pop and I could hear shoes on the kitchen tile floor. I thought it was my Dad's friend and yelled, Don't come up here!

Why? Jamie said.

Oh my God, Jamie, is that you? You have to come up here.

What is this shit in the pot?

Jamie, I can't do it, you have to help me. I had the bathroom door open and I was leaning just my neck and head out of it. He was still standing down in the kitchen.

I'm waxing my bikini, I yelled. I've got wax all over one side and I can't pull it off, I'm too scared.

No.

Please!

I could hear his feet on the stairs. Slow, like in a suspense movie.

I'm covering my eyes, he said. I don't want to see myself do this.

Just one toe and a hand came into the bathroom. Where are you? Jamie said.

I was standing with one foot inside the bathtub and one foot out of it, on the linoleum floor. I had my jeans on only one leg. Jamie felt his way into the room with one hand trailing along the wall.

This is the worst thing I have ever done, he said.

No it's not, I said. Pull!

He still had his hand over his eyes, but with the fingers apart, like a kid who is cheating at hide and seek.

You're fucking it up, I said.

I said, Man up, please. Pull out my pubic hair and I'll make you a Bloody Caesar.

Jamie took his hand off his face and looked down. He got one hand braced on my hip. Put your leg up on the wall, he said. This is going to work better if I can see what I'm doing.

I put my leg up and he ripped the wax off and I kicked him in the jaw. Sort of by accident.

Sorry, I said. That really hurt.

Jesus, Jamie said. He was on the floor holding on to his jaw. Do you not own a bathing suit?

Hey, I said. That looks pretty good. Maybe we should do the other side so I can match.

You're lucky to have found a guy who'll put up with you, Del said. We were sitting out on a bench on Yonge Street. It was me and him and Jamie. A group of pigeons were hanging around, trying to look nonchalant but really waiting for us to drop food. They were like a bunch of guys leaning on a bar, pretending not to look at the blonde girl who just walked in. There were maybe six of them. The street smelled a lot like pigeon. Del and I were on our lunch break. I think Jamie was hanging out with us just so he could tell the waxing story.

You're not telling this story to anyone else, are you? I said. Because I think most girls go to a professional.

Del picked at a crumb on his wrist. He was eating plain crackers. You could really see all the bones and veins in the back of his hand. They snagged off each other as he moved. It looked like it hurt to use his hands.

He said, If I were a guy, I would have told you to fuck off a long time ago.

You *are* a guy, I said.

And yet you've never asked me to wax your twat.

That's what makes me so special, Jamie said. He straightened a pretend bow tie.

You know, I said, in only a few short months I will be gone from this city and the two of you will have nothing left to laugh about. I had applied only to universities that weren't in Toronto.

I said, You will be reduced to lamentation.

After that they spent the rest of the break pretending to cry whenever they talked to me.

Just you wait, I said to Jamie. You can barely cope when I go away for the weekend.

I wasn't sure if this was true, but it was how I liked to think of him. I felt the same way when he had to wait for me to get ready to go out somewhere, or to close up the store at the end of the night. Sometimes I found a few little extra jobs to do, to slow myself down. You know you're in a very safe place when someone is sitting in a chair and complaining at you to hurry up. I said, You're going to miss me like crazy. You don't even know.

Sniff, Jamie said. Sniff, sniff.

There was a place on Charles Street where we liked to drink coffee. It was the end of May and the sun was finally good enough. If you wore black, you could sit outside and feel really warm. We got the coffee in styrofoam cups and walked down Yonge past a strip club. There were a lot of full colour pictures in the window. You know. For promotional reasons. Jamie said he knew a girl who worked there.

She's a university student, he said. She's only dancing for the money.

He pointed to her picture. She's a really nice girl, he said.

I told him some good stories about parties he'd missed. I'd been to an acid party where a guy I knew showed up wearing a purple velvet suit. He was head-to-toe electric purple. Everyone threw stuff at him, I said. They threw stuff at him until he left. One girl cried and everything. I don't know why you never come out with me.

What about Ponyboy? Jamie said. He meant Max.

What about him? I said.

The guy's a superfreak, I'm not going if he's there.

Oh for fuck's sake.

I don't care if you fuck him, do whatever you want. I just don't want to talk to him. Guy's got nothing to say.

I'm not even fucking him anymore, I told you that.

I mashed up my empty cup and threw it at a garbage can on the street. The can was already full and my cup rolled around on the top of it and then fell on the ground.

Jamie had come out to Larissa's for only one poker game, back in the winter when Max and I were still seeing each other. I'd gone downstairs for a bit with Max, and Jamie claimed to have overheard us having sex. On the way home he kept smacking his hands together to make a slapping sound and shouting, What was this? What was this?

The air was cold and his hands got redder and redder.

I didn't mind so much just walking down Avenue Road, but when the bus came I told him to knock it off. I was never going to be able to live that one down and yet here was Jamie, clearly in love with a stripper, and did I say one word about that?

We went into an art store. I was looking for a print to bring with me to school, something I'd seen in one of the books Jamie had given me. There was a copy in a store uptown but it was more than I could afford. Down here near the art college we found a much smaller version, almost postcard-sized. Grasset's "La Morphinomane." A hooker shooting up, Jamie said. Very nice. Good first impression for the new roommate. He leaned around me and thumbed through the rest of the prints in the same bin. His chin was on my shoulder.

I liked her. I liked the way her hair licked back off her face. I liked the face: its mix of apprehension and anticipation, ecstasy and disgust.

By the middle of summer, I couldn't wait to leave home. Del had split with Jeff and was living in a little loft in the Junction. I liked to go there and sit in the alcove in behind his bed and look out the giant windows and watch the freight trains with all their green and black and red cars go by. I brought my Grasset print with me to show Del and he told me where to have it framed for cheap. I was working full-time at the store, but my money was supposed to be for school.

I'm booked into a room at Casey House, Del said. They put me on their list.

We were drinking green tea with maple syrup stirred in. I had brought over some soup in a stainless steel bowl and Del put it in the fridge.

Casey House is a place for people who are dying. Del was a person I liked to go to lunch with. When you're eighteen, everyone you know is talking about the beginning of their life. What people are talking about is the city they want to live in, or when they can borrow a car and drive you to Ikea to look for a mirror. Del gave me a lot of details about how a hospice works. There are two kinds of beds: respite beds and palliative beds. A respite bed is one you get to stay in for a couple of weeks, until you're well enough to go home. A palliative bed is different.

Three months to go! Del said. He smiled like he was a tap dancer or something. He'd shaved off his muttonchops because he thought his hair was getting thin and he didn't want to look like a hag, but without the sideburns his face was hard and yellow. He smelled like brown vitamin pills.

That's morbid, I said. Stop that. Isn't there something about a positive attitude keeping you healthy?

Casey House was famous because Princess Diana had just spent some time there while she was on a visit to Canada. There was a picture of her on the cover of the *Sun* talking to a man in a wheelchair. He had a plaid blanket on his lap and Diana was sitting in front of a stained glass window. From the outside it just looked like a nice old house.

When he was younger, Del had studied art in Morocco and also had some wild times there. His studio was full of stacked paintings of bodies. I stood up and picked at the canvases. Some of his Morocco stories were really good.

What did you tell your parents? I said. Aren't they going to wonder where you are?

Pneumonia, Del said. You'd be surprised how much trouble I have with pneumonia.

And they believe that?

Del had his hands wrapped around the tea cup to keep them warm.

When I was a kid, he said, they sent me to boarding school. I used to bring friends home for the weekend. My mother would find globs of spunk in the carpet and we'd tell her the dog puked.

Trust me, Del said. If she wanted to know the truth, we would have started talking a long time ago.

Del had been sick the whole time I knew him. I never knew him when he didn't take a ton of pills every day, or when he wasn't waiting for his boyfriend to get sick too.

Outside the window it was bright and cloudless. I wanted to be on the highway with my thumb out, wearing a cowboy hat and peeing in gas stations. I wanted to feel like everything I owned could fit on my body. There was a collective anxiety among eighteen-year-olds. Larissa went down to the States to see a Grateful Dead show and didn't came back. After three weeks her father found her in a parking lot in Kentucky. She was supposed to be working at a nursing home, mopping floors and being cheerful so the old people wouldn't kill themselves.

I told this story to everyone I knew, but then in August I went to France for two weeks with all the money I was supposed to be saving for school. I pretended not to speak any English, and I brought all my best clothes with me in case I got discovered. It was the kind of plan you make when you're fifteen. Sometimes I just sat on trains all day. I wore a big backpack and ended up sleeping in my clothes. I was really afraid of bed bugs.

When I got back, Del was much skinnier. He had a gap between his two front teeth like Lauren Hutton, and the thinner he got, the more you noticed it.

I came out to the Junction and buzzed for him to let me in. His voice was chopped up through the intercom. He sounded like china figures getting knocked off a shelf. When he put his hand up on the doorframe to steady himself, his wrists were twice the size of mine but the skin shrank away from his fingernails. He looked like he was wearing a costume underneath his clothes. He looked like he was made of heavy, heavy bones.

Del sat down on the floor and I opened the fridge. My bowl of soup was still in there and I poured it down the sink. I had to press my lips in and hold my breath to stop myself smelling it as it went down. A thin layer of congealed fat had settled on the top, with some mould growing on top of it. Bits of old chicken got caught in the drain with the fat and mould and Del didn't have any rubber gloves so I had to use my hands to scoop it out and throw it away. He had a bar of yellow laundry soap on the edge of the sink and I scrubbed my hands three times under hot, hot water, until they were all red and the cuticles were tearing away. Del's eyes were closed.

I didn't have anything to give him. I was leaving home for good and moving to a new town a couple hours up the 401. I didn't have a car of my own and I wouldn't have come back every weekend, anyway.

Jamie put his head next to mine and stretched his arm way out, camera in hand. We were on the boardwalk near the white Humber bridge, drinking lemonade and eating french fries. It was Labour Day weekend, so once the sun went down we knew we were going to be cold. We'd rollerbladed down from his house and made it to the east end and back but it had taken all afternoon. We liked to set these challenges for ourselves: Ashbridge's to the Humber, how long does that take? Jamie was staying in Toronto for school. I could have gone to Ryerson with him. I wanted to leave.

We were talking about where I'd be living, in residence. It's like an old house, I said. Half the people who live there are international students, and half aren't.

What do you count as? Jamie asked and I said, Shut up.

I was going to do a Master's degree in Senegal when all this was done, and write a thesis on griots.

You just want to hook up with some African poet, Jamie said.

So not true, I said. You don't even know me. You don't know one thing about me.

It was a little bit true. That summer when I was alone in Paris, I'd sat in a stairwell with a sculptor from Ivory Coast for about eleven minutes. His skin was almost blue and he had red, red eyes.

I told Jamie, I've never seen eyes that red before. I don't know where the stairs led to. They went down underground off the square at Les Halles. So, anyway, I don't need to go to Senegal to hook up with some poet. Already done.

Really I hadn't done much more than sit there and look at him, but Jamie didn't need to know that. The man's hands had felt rough against my face. After a few minutes I decided that I was probably making a mistake of some kind and I got up and walked away. Ivory Coast followed behind me for a while before giving up. Jamie knew plenty of stories that ended this way so I didn't bother telling him all the details.

What about Ryerson? I asked.

There's a juried art show in the fall, Jamie said. I'm putting your Bernardo picture in.

Jamie was going to be a photojournalist. He'd had to submit a portfolio and everything. Some of the pictures in the portfolio were of me, because he was always hauling his camera around with us. In one of the pictures I'm standing in an art gallery. Behind me on the wall are artful photographs of murderer's houses, including the one where Paul Bernardo lived with his wife Karla, down in St.

Catherines. I'm laughing and looking really natural because Jamie had lied and said he was just testing his light meter.

If I had known there were to be photographs, I said, I would never have worn my glasses. I was wearing my glasses, for crying out loud. I would have put them in my pocket.

I said, You're a fucking traitor.

That made Jamie really happy, like there wasn't a better compliment. He went around eating his french fries out of a carton in a really light-hearted way after I said that.

The day before I left for school I took Del out to Cherry Beach. I picked him up in my mother's car. On the way down the stairs, I held his elbow. He was moving pretty slow, and I wanted to make sure he didn't fall. The elbow seemed like a good, non-patronizing body part to hold. I had an old cough drop tin with a couple of pinners in it that Jamie had made for me. Del stopped feeling so nauseous when he was high. It was raining and I suggested that we just sit and hotbox the car but Del wanted to walk down to the water. I gathered up the change that I had sitting in the cup holder and stuffed it into my pockets. I always keep a bunch of loonies in there for parking meters, but my father has this thing about crackheads breaking into the car if they see any money lying around. The crackheads are going to steal my loonies.

Hey baby, want to steal my loonies?

See? You can make anything sound dirty. That was the kind of joke Del used to like, but I didn't have time to tell it. He was already out of the car. The beach was all pebbles instead of sand: pebbles and used condoms and old needles. There was something about the way Del moved that reminded me of a bird. Not a graceful bird, like a heron or an eagle. The kind of bird that can't fly and has to negotiate its legs around everything. His knees were really high up and he was taking all his steps sideways. He had a giant umbrella and looked like a mushroom. I ran after him in my rainboots and we smoked the joints sitting on a big wet rock.

Just a few weeks to go, Del said.

No way! I said. It'll get better again, you'll see. I dug around in my pockets. I said, I'll bet you everything I've got on me that you go to respite and come out again just fine.

I had six dollars and Del thought that was really funny. His cheekbones were like coat hangers. It was the best bet I could make. I threw the money into my cough drop tin and closed it up and stuck it in his pocket. His jacket was hanging loose and he clinked and clanked all the way back to the car, the tin bumping against his hip.

In the car he put his hand over mine. I had already started the engine and was about to throw it into reverse. He was looking out the window, away from me and I knew I should take the hand. In the last few months Del had developed a rash that wouldn't go away. The back of his hand looked like it was covered with mosquito bites that were scabbing over. I tried to remember if I'd cut my own hand recently. It was the first time I'd ever been afraid of him. I didn't say anything or do anything nice, I just drove. I figured letting him hold onto my hand with me not holding his back was the best I could do.

When I walked him back up the stairs to his loft, I cradled one arm around his whole body so he wouldn't lose his balance. He felt like a bag of things you donate to the food bank, like everything he was made of was heavy, but loose. Like the inside parts of him were rolling around and if he fell, they might tip out. There was something about this that made me feel like a little kid. I wanted things to be opposite:

I wanted him to hold me up, instead. Thinking like that made me so guilty and ashamed that I hurried him up the stairs even faster. I couldn't wait to shut the door. I wanted Del and his six-loonie tin on one side, and me on the other.

I meant to drive straight home. I was leaving in the morning and still had packing to do. But what I did was drive to Jamie's house. I rapped on his basement window and tracked mud all over the carpet down into his room. I couldn't even cry. He pulled off my clothes, one piece at a time, with his good, clean hands.

I thought everything at home would stay frozen if I didn't go looking for news. When I came home for my birthday and Thanksgiving, I only stayed two nights. I didn't want to be there for any more than the minimum necessary time. Then it was December. I hadn't heard from Del in three months.

The billboards on Yonge Street hadn't even changed. I was almost surprised the weather was so cold. The day after Christmas I went out drinking with Larissa and some other people I knew. I rode home on Brett Furnival's shoulders. We passed the bookstore and I pointed. I used to work there, I said. I worked there for a long time. It was about two in the morning. All the lights were down in every store window on the street. Something flashed at me from the bookstore: the streetlamp was reflecting off a Christmas ornament hanging in the doorway. I had a sudden, terrible feeling. I realized for the first time how long I'd been gone. It felt as though my throat were being wrung out.

I climbed down off Brett's shoulders. I fell off. I was in a big hurry and didn't want too many questions. It wasn't snowing. The air was too cold to carry anything in it, even a tiny thing like a snowflake. I pressed my face against the smooth glass of the window. I thought if I did that, the lights inside would go on and everything would be there, laid out like a feast. I thought I would see myself on the top of a rolling ladder, counting overstock.

The cold in the glass made my cheekbone ache. A few cars drove by. Their headlights flashed and then the store was black inside. You couldn't even see the shadows of things.

One good thing about a city is that there are always so many other people around, distracting you with their noise and their craziness, singing and begging and fighting, that you never really have a quiet moment to stop and think. I didn't think at all about where I was going. I just went. It was warmer in the subway. I got off at Dundas West and walked down Roncesvalles. There was a Chinese woman standing on her porch, smoking a cigarette. It was the middle of the night. She was the only person I'd seen for three blocks.

Good! Good! she shouted. Only good things for you! She said my aura looked really orange.

In Jamie's driveway I knelt down and rapped on the basement window. I wasn't sure he'd be awake and I lay down on the concrete. It had been shovelled dry, but there was some built-up ice along the edges. The ice had a sharp look, as though someone had tried chipping away at it with a heavy implement. I closed my eyes and decided it would be okay to go to sleep there until Jamie came out to get me. There were bits of gravel or road salt digging into my scalp and my wrist where it stuck out of my coat sleeve. It was a small, irritating kind of pain and I found it comforting. The screen door made a noise.

I could see Jamie's bare feet. He was wearing a pair of old jeans and no shirt. His hair looked ragged, but only on one side. He didn't look like he'd been sleeping; he looked wrinkled, like he'd been rolled up and stretched out again. I sat up. The lights in the basement were all on.

Why are you on the ground? he said.

I need to come in for a while.

I thought you fell. Are you okay?

I was resting.

Now's not a really good time.

I said, I never heard from Del. I lifted one arm in the air and waited for Jamie to help pull me up. He rubbed his hands against his jeans and looked over his shoulder.

I pushed against the wall and stood up on my feet.

You can't come in right now, he said.

Did you hear what I said?

I just can't.

Jamie. I took a step toward him and put my hand on his waist. All the fine hairs on his stomach were standing up in the cold. Please, I said.

What do you think, he said. Look. Del died, like, a month ago. You weren't around.

I left you messages, he said. You wouldn't even call me back. Fuck it's cold out here.

I took my hand off him and started walking down the drive. He was standing there holding the screen door open and then he let it close behind him.

I'm sorry about Del, he shouted after me. I really am. I'm really sorry.

Fuck you, I called out. I didn't turn around. I made sure my voice was full of sunshine.

The houses in that neighbourhood are brick and red or yellow or white, with tall stairs. Some people had left their Christmas lights on and the places where the bulbs had gone out were like icing that's been licked away. I stood out on the corner next to the traffic light.

I thought of sitting in the playground with just the dark and the stars until the sun came up. I thought of walking down to where the pond is and sliding out until the ice got chunky and soft, where the reeds are. Jamie and I used to walk home through the park at night because his mother told us not to. There was some change in my pocket and I counted it out and looked to see if any of the dimes were subway tokens.

The Chinese lady was still out on her porch. A ledge ran along the sidewalk. It reminded me of a balance beam, but it was covered in ice. The frost was shiny. It looked like something you want to eat. I thought about my orange aura, how good that must be.

AJACCIO BELONGED TO THE GENOESE

When they met he followed her up the street on his knees, screaming in English, Hello, I Love You. Hands knitted together. The cuffs of his pants ragged. Carla's fingers against the hem of her skirt, holding it still as she walked ahead of him. The skirt too short now that she had a man crawling after her. Nico paid her way onto the metro, followed her all the way to Joliette. At the end of her street Carla turned to him and said finally Go home, go home. Please. I'm not allowed to go out with foreigners and he slapped his hands to his sides: What are you talking about? I am French and we are in France!

Her mother calling out to her from the open window. Nico said, In Marseille thirty percent claim Italian heritage! I am probably Italian, too! and Carla slipped inside to hang up her coat, then went into the bathroom and sat down on the toilet, sweating.

He bought her *langoustes*. Fat ones, claws snapping, and when she said What will I do with these? Carry them in my purse? he took her home to his house and set them free on the kitchen counter, watched to see if they would fight. I can't bear to cook them, Carla said. Imagine being boiled alive. Their tails skittering against the slick countertop. We could make them race? Nico said and Carla shook her head very fast. They filled the soup pot with cold water, added salt, and let the langoustes swim. Sitting out in the courtyard smoking cigarettes with the pot between them on the ground until the neighbour came by and shouted at them that These are not pets! Floating a little parsley in the water to be the seaweed.

They bought a disposable camera from a street vendor and took all the pictures in twenty minutes, Nico pulling her against him, one arm stretched out to click the shutter. Strangers in the background. Just Carla, lying in the walkway, shoes and feet all around her. Just Nico, but the camera shifted. His ear, his left ear and shoulder. His striped shirt.

Sleeping in his parents' bed when they were away for the weekend in Antibes or Carcassonne, sunlight entering the room so early through thin white curtains. Old people like to get up in the morning, Nico said. Carla filled the bathtub and lay back with the door locked.

I can see you through the crack! Nico on the other side. The keyhole.

She had once peered through the little hole in the door herself and watched his mother remove a tampon, one hand groping between her legs, so she knew he was telling her the truth. She blew soap bubbles from her fist and they came to rest on the side of the tub like the bulbous heads of jellyfish, pink and trembling.

All that time her father was in the hospital. The grandmother came from Bolzano to help, driving herself across the border and through Monaco in a blue Citroën, arriving with boxes of tomatoes in jars and two suitcases of straight dresses and kerchiefs to wear over her hair, to hide the thin patches. She moved into Carla's room and slept in Carla's bed. Carla was given a new mattress on the floor. The grandmother snored and kept her things all over the room: night cream, her teeth in a glass on the dresser. Nico wanted to come to La Joliette, to meet the grandmother and the mother, but Carla said No. Because I'm not Italian? he said and Carla bit her lip.

Nobody would really care. The grandmother herself from Südtirol. Carla couldn't explain. It was just a feeling she had. Nico belonged in the Panier, in the Vieux Port, in Noailles; Carla squirmed in her seat on the metro, on her way to see him. She laughed so that her lower lip wouldn't shake. How could she manage with him sitting at her mother's long wooden table, eating cookies at Christmastime?

Her father had fallen off some scaffolding when he was working. Now he was learning to walk in a *clinique* in Vitrolles. It will not be easy, the doctor said. It will not go fast. The doctor's name was Armand Gainsbourg. (Probably a Jew, said Carla's mother, when he was out of the room. They like to do that, change their name and make it French. His name is Ginsburg. She unwrapped a candy and popped it into her mouth, crunching loudly.) This learning to walk will take months, said Armand Gainsbourg. The muscles are in atrophy. New connections must be forged between the legs and the brain. The grandmother stayed on. More boxes of her things arrived by post, sent by a sister in Italy. There was almost no room for all these things in the little house. Carla could barely see the floor tiles around her mattress.

When she was eight, and they were still living in Genoa, she once saw her cousin suffocate a rabbit. He did it with a pair of socks, balled up the toe end of one by stuffing the other one deep inside it, and slipped the whole thing over the rabbit's head. It was a pet rabbit that belonged to a younger cousin. It lived in a cage on the floor of her bedroom. The suffocating took a long time, the rabbit beating its head against the metal of the cage, trying to release itself from the sock. Probably it would have survived if it hadn't spent so much energy on trying to get free.

They were playing hide and go seek. Carla was in the closet and her cousin came in with the socks. Then he left. She crouched on the closet floor, one hand on the doorknob. What should she do? If she nipped out for just a moment, she could free the rabbit's nostrils. But what if she were caught? Finally it lay down. Carla was relieved. It's always comfortable to have a decision, one way or another.

They talked about getting married. Or, Carla did. Nico refused to discuss a future tense with her so long as she refused to bring him to her family, and Carla wouldn't, so things stayed as they were. They would have had a long time to wait, anyway. His parents were the kind that believed in school. Everyone in Nico's family was a doctor or a professor. He had a cousin who lived in Corsica and studied nurse sharks. He was the leading expert on the Mediterranean nurse shark, and spent half his life in scuba gear. Nico liked the idea of the scuba gear part, but was unsettled on just what he might study while he was down there. He preferred fishing, but the good permits are all handed down between family members, fishing families, and who wants to work for nothing? He was one of those men who carry a salt taste on their skin. Even when he hadn't been swimming for days, there was a lick of brine on him. Just from living next to the sea all his life. You could run your tongue along his jaw and the salt would make it burn.

He stole some codeine from his work. On weekends he was the night janitor at a medical clinic in Noailles and wore those baggy blue pants and v-necked shirts they give to orderlies in hospitals. Keys on a chain that stretched from his pocket to the belt loop of the pants. Carla took the metro up there early on Saturday mornings, in time to catch him as he got off, and they stopped in the market next to the station and bought dates or honey pastries from an Algerian baker he knew.

Nico lived with his family in the quartier Panier, up the hill from the old port, in a house that used to be a convent in the middle ages. So said the mother. No one was home and they sat in armchairs by the window and Nico said, I didn't know you were coming over tonight. Over and over. He'd taken three of the codeine tablets, washed them down with a few beers. He let his head rest against the back of the chair. Carla sat with her legs crossed and one arm over her body, fingering her elbow. Her thin cardigan was too hot, even at night. He'd given her some beer in a glass, but no coaster. There was a ring of condensation on the windowsill where she set the glass.

In the doorway she had tried to kiss him, urgently she thought, pushing her tongue against his, but his legs were like jelly and he had to go and sit down. His feet stuck out over the carpet, cigarette ash falling from his hand and his laughing mouth as he smoked. Now she crawled over to him and undid his belt buckle and put her mouth on him and he laughed and laughed and told her he loved her, just like that. His penis lying there like a bit of old rag.

She went home, all the way to La Joliette, to her parents'

new stucco home that smelled of garlic and bread, on the metro by herself, and wasn't afraid even when a pock-marked Arab followed her down the tunnel, yelling I can see your panties! Thinking of the damp piece of rag in his own pants. At home she told her mother she'd been to the cinema and nobody asked her what she'd seen, or with whom. She was eighteen. High school was over.

Her father was in training all week in Vitrolles. They have me on a treadmill day and night, he told Carla, and described to her the metal helmet he wore during these training sessions. To stimulate the brain, he said. Fried brains! I like them better with bacon. They sat outside in the garden, on a bench, so they could smoke. Carla liked to sneak in a little grappa in a flask, even though they gave the father some wine with his lunch and dinner. It was the least she could do. He seemed to have shrunk since the accident, the skin over his cheeks going grey the way you might expect hair to change colour. His hair was the only thing that remained the same, thick and black. He kept a fine-toothed silver comb the length of Carla's index finger in his shirt pocket, and a barber came into the *clinique* every three weeks and gave him a trim. He'd once had forearms like boards.

In Genoa, he built a living room playhouse for Carla from scrap lumber he dragged home from his work on construction sites, while the mother lodged a loud complaint with Mary and the Holy Trinity in the next room: he was taking up half the apartment! The playhouse was quite small, with just enough room for Carla to climb in and peep out the window he'd left her, and he gave her an espresso cup from the cabinet (porcelain! wailed the mother) out of which she drank apricot juice or tiny amounts of raspberry syrup stirred into soda water. They passed the cup between them through the window, the father adding spoonfuls of syrup and water from the siphon on the kitchen table. The heads of the nails he'd used were embossed with a triangle pattern, the logo of the nail company. By pressing very hard, Carla could force the triangle to come up red on the soft flesh of her thumbs.

Her job was at a nursery school not far from the Vieux Port. Wiping noses and bums, the mother said, but Carla liked the scent the children carried with them, all of them smelling slightly of spoilt milk, or yeast. They were warm and growing, like dough held beneath a cloth. The hair on their heads a little damp from play. Together they squished clay, or spread paint with their fingers. She let them play with dry macaroni—better than sand, because it doesn't matter if they put it in their mouths.

Three year old Agnès cried every morning when her mother left. There was something in the crying that Carla found furtively enjoyable, a feeling she got in her teeth, her gumline, when the child wailed. In the afternoon, if she were feeling sleepy, Carla would say things to Agnès to make her cry again: I'm going to lock you in the closet with the brooms until the dustman comes and finds you, or, If you can't go pee in the toilet right now I'm going to pinch you. Afterwards she felt guilty. But it was so good to comfort, to make it better.

Nico's house was like water to her. Even her eyes felt cool and slick. Couldn't I just live here? she asked him. She wanted to know when his parents would be going away for the summer. Would they go to Paris in August, or further?

Bruges? Geneva?

What will you tell your family? Nico asked her. Where will you say you are going?

Carla wrapped herself in his mother's towels, tied his mother's scarves around her neck.

You look like a stewardess, Nico said. They were talking in the front hall of the house before going out. If Carla stood in just the right place, she could face him and still see herself reflected in the dark pane of the window. She told him Agnès was no longer coming to the little school. She'd been in a car accident with her mother, and her collarbone was broken. This was the truth. Nico crouched down to lace his boots. In the window, the reflected Carla watched him suck on the frayed ends of the laces and then thread them through each hole. He tied them in double knots. She watched herself standing over him. Agnès *had* been in an accident. Carla had seen the doctor's letter herself, where it was tucked away in the filing cabinet, but somehow she couldn't shake the feeling that the mother was covering for her, that Carla herself had hurt the girl. That once, in a state of unawareness, she really had pinched her, too hard, and now Agnès couldn't come back to school because Carla could not be trusted.

They drove along the coast to Cannes and then north, in the white Renault. Taking country roads so they wouldn't have to pay tolls. Nico shifting down to take the curves. Instead of the brake, he said. Like this. His hand now over Carla's. Up onto the Moyenne Corniche, tight against the cliffs, half way up the mountain. Moyenne. Half way. On the lower roads: keen, white church steeples sticking up out of villages. Way down, the sea, and then only that. Whitecaps like trails of dust in the sunlight.

He stopped the car on the runoff and they walked back to the roadside and stood on the edge, the backs of their knees pressed against the barrier and the trucks speeding around the bend and skimming their bodies. I can't fight the wind, Carla said.

See the face on that one! Nico's own broad face, chipped tooth showing, yelling and shouting at Carla. The sudden terror in the drivers' eyes as they came around the curve and saw Nico and Carla standing there on the painted line at the edge of the road. Carla with her fingertips resting on her thighs, eyes closed, hair drifting across her face. The insides of her eyelids brilliant, shadows like birds or angels speeding through them.

The cars were coming down off the Grande Corniche, higher and more serpentine above. We could keep going, Nico said.

What, to Italy? Carla turned around and locked her kneecaps against the concrete block. The side of the mountain ran down, broken, to Beaulieu below her. Its severity hidden beneath patches of scrub and sage. If I fell, thought Carla. The rock face like steps. It would be like a doll thrown from the second floor down to the first; I'd be like a doll. She grabbed at Nico's hand, his shoulder. It's not falling if you mean to do it.

The first time they had sex was not Carla's first time. They were in the damp grass in the Parc Valmer at night, Carla's stomach slapping as she fell onto him. Later she told him her first time had been in the front seat of a car the year before, in Italy. The boy hadn't known anything about condoms, but Carla insisted. She'd learned about them in school. He must have done something wrong, Carla said, because I found the condom three days later. It was riding around in me all that time. You could have been pregnant, Nico said. The idea was amusing to him. You would have a baby sucking on your tits right now! Maybe I still would have fucked you, though, and Carla hit him and hit him with her shoe: No! No you couldn't!

On the day her father came home and sat in his wheelchair by the window, sipping from Carla's flask, she and Nico went back to the same park. The treatments had failed. They lay down on the steps of the villa and listened to the gulls and the cars sweeping along on the road above them, Carla swelling up with a quiet rage that was like mud, heavy in all her joints. Nico had the chance to go to Corsica and work for his cousin as a diver. Carla could come along and live on an island. The town, Ajaccio, used to belong to the Genoese, Nico said. The French and the Genoese have been passing it back and forth for centuries. What could be more perfect?

They lay there on their backs and got cold. It was November. When she was sure that Nico was asleep, Carla went home. It was almost morning. She was sitting alone in the metro and stood up to look through the window into the next car, to see if there was anyone there or if she was the only one, maybe the only one on the whole train. But there were people there, a man and a woman. The woman was crying and bent at the waist, her arms wrapped around her stomach. Carla imagined that the place on her body where she was holding her stomach was a seam. If she let go, her body would fall away into two halves. The man was standing up. When he saw Carla he bent over the woman and put his hands on her face and twisted her head around to make her look at Carla, too. The woman stopped moving and sat there, with the man's hands, one on either side of her face, and stared at Carla with big, blank eyes. She stopped crying. It was like she couldn't believe anyone else could exist like that, watching her cry through a window. The next stop was Joliette and Carla got off. She walked home with just the beginning of light like a slit vein running along the horizon, bleeding up.

She went into the kitchen and sliced off big hunks of bread and ate them with butter and ham and cheese on a plate, just taking one bite after another, then more bread, this time with jam. She drank two glasses of wine. She'd been up all night. She was that hungry.

All this six years ago, the last time they were together. Carla left to work for her own cousin, waiting tables in Capri and came back to Marseille only when she was sure Nico had stopped looking for her, gone for good to Corsica. She brought a friend of a friend home with her and married him. He agreed to move, even though he didn't speak the language and didn't like to leave his mother.

Last month, Carla's friend Odile called to say she had seen Nico, asleep in his car, while on a business trip in Toulouse. She first recognized the car, the white Renault, splotches of rust along the driver's door panel covered over with duct tape to stop it spreading. I didn't think it could be him, she said. I mean, the same car? He was parked in a side street near her hotel with the window down and his seat leaning slightly back. His mouth hanging open as he slept.

That's when I knew, she said. His chipped tooth, right in front. Exactly the same.

It wasn't much of a chip, thought Carla. Sour that she hadn't been in Toulouse to see this, had instead been home hand-straining peas to feed the baby. He'd damaged the tooth when she knew him, playing soccer. It wasn't as bad as some she'd seen, front teeth broken in half and capped. The ball had bounced up hard and Nico tried to take it on his chin, but misjudged. His right front tooth. Just a sliver gone, a shard of glass, sharp against Carla's tongue. A pinch in her lip, or the tips of her nipples.

EVERYTHING UNDER YOUR FEET

For one whole year I did nothing but run up a mountain. In the morning I would get up, brush my teeth and put on my running shoes. I didn't even drink a cup of coffee. The mountain was right outside my back door, so I didn't have far to go to get to work. I didn't have to commute. What I did all day was commute.

That year I lived in a small town called Winsome's View. There was no good reason for me to live there. It wasn't a place where I had any family or friends. I had a Master's degree in philology. My parents were convinced this had something to do with speaking a lot of languages and wanting to help people. At graduation my mother gripped my shoulders and whispered, Your whole life's in front of you!

This alarmed me. I looked up, possibility whipping out from my body like an endless bolt of cloth.

They handed me a gas card loaded with two hundred dollars and my name, Lydia Strunk, stamped on it. I drove. It was the end of springtime. Everything made my eyes hurt. When the money was gone, and the gas was gone, there was the mountain and the house at the bottom of it. I tried to coast the car toward the driveway, but the road levelled out and I lost momentum. I ended up on the soft shoulder. The landlord handed me the house keys and an open bucket of road salt. He had a patched-up hole in his neck and had to speak through a microphone device that he held to the hole. He always carried extra batteries in his breast pocket, and he yelled instructions as I unpacked. No pets, he said. No babies!

In Winsome's View, you either worked at the automotive factory in the next town or you stayed home all day wearing track pants. There was a tire fire on the edge of town that had been burning for over two years solid. Two guys were employed by the township to try to control the tire fire. They wore brown overalls and pitched shovelfuls of loose dirt against the smoky places. The first time I walked by, they called out to me. Hey you slut! they yelled. They yelled out to anyone passing by. It didn't matter if you were a woman or a man. Everyone was a slut to them.

Almost the whole rest of the town drove the fifteen clicks to the factory. It was the kind of factory that made little parts for other factories to turn into real cars. The first morning, I opened my curtains and watched a chain of fenders stretching down the two lane road that led from Winsome's View to the factory town: those were the day shift workers. All that was left in the houses were fat women and babies. The highway cut straight through the centre of town with all the grubby front lawns sidling up to it. Out my front window I could see a row of round faces looking back at me from inside their own windows across the street. Out my back window was the mountain.

There was a downtown with a few stores but I never went there. I only went downtown if I had to buy supplies: macaroni, canned spinach, that soup with the tiny meatballs in it. I had an entire house to myself. I measured the rooms by stretching out on the floor and multiplying by the length of my body. Like this: Bedroom = Me x Me-and-a-Half. Kitchen = Two-Me x Three-Me-and-a-Quarter. I didn't have a radio or a record player. I wished I could dance and practiced kicking into handstands against the empty dining room wall. There were bits of leftover plastic wrap around the windows where the last tenant had tried to keep the drafts out. For a week I lay in bed at night, peeling strips of it off the window frame. It flaked into my fingers like rough pastry.

I found an old pair of running shoes in the road. I was the one in the road; the running shoes were hanging from the telephone wire above me. I'd been leaning on the car as though it might go somewhere. There was the roar of an airplane overhead. I squinted up, but everything was washed out. All you could see was the sun-white sky. Ceiling unlimited. Below the sky was the mountain, jagged and bushy and dimensional. I stood on top of the car with my feet wide against the roof racks and untied the shoes and they fit. I didn't have a job, just the gas card with nothing on it. I jumped down off the roof and set my hands on the hatch of the car and rocked it until it rolled off the shoulder. Then I started pushing. I had to run a few steps up the driver's side, so I could push with one hand and stick the other hand through the window to steer. I thought I'd push the car all the way into town, or into a pond if I could find one. On my way down the road a man named Frank Rooster came along in a yellow tow truck. Frank Rooster owned the gas station. I only know this because the tow truck said Frank Rooster, Gas & Autobody on the side of it. We didn't talk to each other at all. He slowed down and looked at me from inside his truck window and then he stopped and got out. I stopped pushing and took my hands off the hood. I looked down at my feet with my new running shoes on them. Then I turned my body back toward the mountain.

Sorry, car, I said. Shoes = running.

The first trip up the mountain was slow going. Any paths were rough-worn and full of switchbacks. It was like you had to climb the mountain twice to climb it once. I had a little running experience from my high school track team. I knew you had to land lightly on your feet. I knew you couldn't make a fist. If you make a fist, all your energy rushes down your arms and out your fingers like electric eels. Everything about running is about care. You can't just hurtle yourself through the bush. You have to pretend you are holding onto a potato chip in each hand and you can't break them. You have to run as if you believe that everything under your feet is something alive and living and if you're not careful you will be a murderer. I pretended that under my feet was a colony of snails that was actually one of the world's great civilizations.

I listened to my own breath. When the slope got steep, I sighed to slow my heart down. There were roots and burrs and sap and sharp things everywhere: it was a forest. I got used to running with my hands up, to protect my eyes. At the top of the mountain, there was an oak tree that had been hit by lightning when it was very young. It was split in two down close to the bottom. Instead of dying, the trunk had scarred in a round way and then kept growing as two limbs that were stuck together. Do you remember all those pictures of Siamese twins joined at the waist? The tree was like that. The branches were two heads that weren't joined.

I circled the tree. I didn't like to let myself rest. The path down was lighter and easier. My body had already swept away the scrub. Gravity lengthened my stride. I closed my eyes. I wasn't afraid of falling.

People asked questions. You know: neighbourhood people. I heard them on the sidewalk when I passed by, or talking loud in their gardens on Saturday mornings as I laced up my shoes. How does she live? they said. Is this some way to make money? They never asked what was at the top of the mountain. They never asked me anything. They assumed I was in training.

I *was* in training. My legs got brown and thin and bramble-scarred. The mountain was my province. I liked the places where thorns and branches had scratched me. The scabs were proof. I was doing something hard. I had a pink Timex stopwatch that I fastened to my shoelace. On the days I ran a little faster, I put ten extra macaronis in my meatball soup. This was like a reward. It was bonus pay. I was the only person in town working the mountain shift. I drew a picture of myself with stick arms and stick legs in front of a big green triangle. I glued it to my kitchen wall. Underneath the picture I wrote "Employee of the Month" in blue magic marker.

Every day, I stepped out of bed and the mountain was still there. The whole summer went by. Across the street, the women in their soft pants watched me from their living room windows. They'd never seen a runner in real life. I caught glimpses of them inside their houses, drinking coffee and vacuuming. I hadn't really talked to another person since I arrived—even the blonde cashier at the grocery store only nodded at my silent purchases. One evening I watched a man push a lawnmower over a pile of raked-up leaves. He was wearing greasy blue work pants and steel-toed boots. Every time he turned the lawnmower around, his wrist flexed and for a moment I could see all the purple veins in the back of his hand. There was a wind and the shredded leaves blew around like loose garbage. I crossed my arms and my fingers were cold against the insides of my elbows. I thought about the cold steel handle of the lawnmower. The man didn't look uncomfortable. His grip never changed.

By the end of October, I had been running up the mountain for almost six months. Cars slowed down whenever they passed my house. Instead of just watching me through the window, families lined the path by my back gate on Sunday mornings. When I came out, some of the children jumped up and down. You'd think the attention would make me feel really important, but it just embarrassed me. It made me want to be the kind of person who doesn't run up a mountain.

What can we do? the people shouted. What do you need?

Some of them had water in Dixie cups that they had brought from their bathroom cup dispensers. They held out the cups as I ran by. If they got too excited, the cups shook and I got wet.

No, no! I said. No, thank you! I don't need any help!

I was really good at running up a mountain.

When I went downtown to buy macaroni or canned spinach, people nodded at me on the street. If I stopped at the corner, waiting for cars to pass, the guys who worked at Frank Rooster's gas station yelled out Hey! Hellooo! and then started jogging on the spot.

Look! they yelled, pointing at their own feet.

Sometimes I tried to smile and sometimes I just looked up at the clouds. I didn't want to seem unpleasant. I didn't want to look like I thought I was hot stuff. My old car was always sitting on the lot and whenever I passed by I whispered to it. Whoa, girl, I'd say. Easy now.

One of the guys had stringy brown hair and a tattoo of a mosquito on his shoulder. The other one wore a name tag that said *Rooster's Autobody—Jeremy Nazdhenko*. I hadn't lived in Winsome's View for very long, so no one knew my name. The gas station guys called me Marathon Girl. It's Marathon Girl! They yelled. Pretty soon other people were yelling out to me too.

My real name seemed very poor in comparison. I didn't correct anyone. Who wants to have a poor name?

One night Jeremy Nazdhenko knocked on the door of my house. He was with his girlfriend. She was wearing tight pink pants and black boots and carrying a picnic basket. They wanted to see me when I wasn't running. I could tell that they wanted to take me out for dinner and drinks and ask me questions and write down all my answers. I didn't open the door, I just called through the keyhole.

I have to get a good night's sleep! I said. Sorry! Some other time!

I had to run up the mountain again in the morning.

Outside it got so cold that I shoved tube socks over my hands to keep them from freezing. While I was running I thought about things you could eat, things other women in Winsome's View ate. I thought about chocolate cake, bruised bananas, stewed raisins. Soft things, sweet things. I rolled the imaginary food around in my mouth with my real tongue. My legs never stopped. Inside me was this raw furnace. It snowed and I sucked the snow in with big, deep gasps until my lungs burned with cold. I remembered being small and seeing pictures of a horse my father had owned before I was born. He let the horse run races in the cold air and its lung froze and it fell down dead. He had a picture of the horse, Jasper, wearing all his racing gear, and another one of Jasper flat out on the ground.

I hadn't knocked more than a minute off my time since the beginning of the fall. On my way to the grocery store, I stopped at Rooster's car lot and sat on my old car's hood. What if I can't get any faster? I asked. I showed the car the insides of my shoes, the places where my feet had worn away the lining, the places that were stained with popped blisters. The car's paint job was stained with kicked-up salt from test drives. Its price was slashed.

Some days I ran sprints up and down the road in front of my house: one hundred metres of long strides, then a loose walk back over the same ground. Children on the sidewalk tried to keep pace, the way Superman runs next to the train.

The burning began to fill my whole body. I was running for six or eight hours every day and timing every trial. Grinding myself down. My face got smaller and smaller. I looked in the mirror and thought, My skull is the size of a child's skull. That night I fell into bed. There was nothing to be done. I didn't work at the factory and I didn't have a baby. I was the Marathon Girl.

One morning in the spring my feet sank into the mud and wouldn't come out. I lost an entire shoe that way. I had to go downtown and buy a new pair of shoes, because no matter what I said the lady wouldn't sell me just one. I even thought she might give me a free shoe. Business had really increased since the town had taken an interest in my running. The window was full of blue t-shirts with the word *Marathon!* written across the front in yellow script. It was Saturday and the store was packed with women buying kids' shirts and matching yellow shoelaces.

You're making me have three shoes! I yelled. Who needs three shoes? I threw my muddy leftover shoe into the window display. It knocked down a child-sized **mannequin.** The child's face was slashed with mud from my shoe. Her wig fell off. This demonstration of power surprised even me. Before I started running up a mountain, I would never have thrown a tantrum in an athletics store. I only watched people like that. Now the bald child mannequin watched me, lying there in her *Marathon!* t-shirt with her face all dirty.

I'm sorry, I whispered to the mannequin. But you were asking for it.

The store lady made a soft fist with her hand at her side. She probably thought I didn't notice. She couldn't kick me out of the store because I was the Marathon Girl.

One day a man was standing at the top of the mountain. Just standing there. He had something cold and black pressed up against his eyes. When I got closer I saw that it was a pair of fold-up binoculars. He was aiming down the trail. There was a copper thermos hanging off a carabiner attached to his belt. He was a red-head and so clean-shaven that his face shone like it was wet. I thought he looked wind-burned from standing there under the sky. He was taller than me by at least a foot. That was the thing that made me step back.

I never stopped when I got to the top. I always just circled the tree and started back down. But the man was standing there and he put the binoculars down on the ground and unscrewed the top of the thermos. He held something out to me. It wasn't a Dixie cup, or even a sports bottle. It was a regular glass made of glass.

Drink this, he said.

I stopped. I drank it.

I know what you're thinking. What if the drink was drugs? Is this Marathon Girl crazy? What if it was poison?

It wasn't. It was carrot juice.

Carrot and celery, the man said. Celery juice, too. That's why it doesn't taste too strong. Do you like it? he said. Why do you run up the mountain?

I still hadn't said a word. I pressed the glass against my lips and teeth.

You must like the view, the man said. We should move your house, he said. We should move your house to the top of the mountain. Then you wouldn't have to run all day.

What are you, I thought, a real estate agent? I didn't say it out loud because I never talk to strangers. Even though in those days I was running up a mountain, I had grown up in a big city where they taught us about strangers.

The man said: I want to run.

I handed him back his glass. He took it from me and his sleeve touched my sleeve. My sleeve was cool and black. It was made of 88% polyester and 12% spandex, which is what we call "technical". Runner's clothes are always made of technical. It wicks.

His sleeve was red and loose, like cinnamon that's been ironed out and stitched into a flag. I thought for a second that if he were cooking in that shirt, leaning over a stove, the loose sleeve might touch the burner and catch fire. For a second I saw his sleeve all kindled and brilliant and my heart started beating. He was on fire and I reached out to touch him and then I was on fire. We were two combustible bodies running through the woods, igniting everything. A jet holocaust. A wheel of flames.

He shifted his feet and put the glass away in his Lewis and

Clark backpack. He screwed the top back on the thermos. I bent down and picked up his binoculars and handed them over. They made a nice clicking sound when they closed up tight. The man attached the binoculars to his belt.

He said, You must be awful afraid to stand still.

I backed up and leaned against the two-headed oak. It was the first really hot day of summer. I wasn't used to stopping halfway: the muscles in my legs felt heavy and worn. Pins and needles in my hands and in my forehead. What I wanted to do was lie down.

I circled the tree. Then I ran back down the mountain.

The next day I woke up and put on my running shoes. I went out in the backyard. The man was there, waiting for me. He was wearing shoes, too: his shoes were black and hard-soled with a thick, silver heel.

Are we going to run up the mountain? he said. I looked at him with just my eyes. I didn't turn my head.

The man lifted his pant legs a little. I twisted my body toward him in case what he was showing me was something dirty. I wouldn't want to miss that. But what he was showing me was his feet and legs. The legs ended underneath the knees and instead of ankles he had metal sticks that sliced down into his shoes. Where his feet should have been curved up nice and flat like ski tips. The sticks were sturdily bolted in.

Have you always had no feet? I said.

Always, the man said. He said his name was Emanuel Brown. He said his mother named him Emanuel because it was like a miracle that he had no feet, especially since his hands were so well formed. Emanuel Brown lifted up a hand and let me take a good look at it. It was soft and pale.

I don't work at the factory, he said. I don't even drive a car.

I don't know about running with no feet, I said.

I think if I ran, Emanuel Brown said, I might start to feel where my feet should be.

I hopped up and down from one foot to the other. It was part of my pre-run ritual.

Do you feel hot where your feet should be? I said. I was thinking of the burning I had inside my body. Maybe soon I would be missing something like Emanuel Brown was missing feet.

No, he said. I feel clean where my feet should be. What I feel where my feet should be is plain white.

I stopped hopping and rubbed my legs a little.

I run up the mountain to get warm, I said.

Are you warm now, Emanuel said, but he wasn't looking at me at all. His eyes were closed. I looked at his red hair and his wet-clean cheeks. I thought he was wearing an earring, but it was a lick of hair that curled under his ear. He wasn't smiling or frowning. His face was nothing. He had a few freckles. You could count them and I did.

I'm so tired, I said.

Okay, I said. Let's run.

We started up the mountain. Emanuel Brown wasn't as slow as I thought he would be. His metal ankles made a clickity-click noise as we ran. We went single file through the bush with me leading. After a while he pushed in front of me. His right arm swung out and held me back at the waist. Everything he did was wrong. He ran with his head down and his fists tight, and he used his shoulders to beat back the overgrowth. He could really move.

It was strange to run with my hands at my sides. I didn't need to protect my face when Emanuel was in front of me.

It almost didn't feel like running. I yelled out instructions from behind.

Turn! I shouted. Left!

I shouted the instructions like he couldn't see the path in front of him. I shouted them loud in case he couldn't hear me in the wind. We got to the top and he didn't stop running. The sky opened up nice and wide over us. The sun was at our backs and burned our shoulders. It made us into stilty, loping shadow runners on the ground. We circled the tree and started back down.

Faster! Emanuel Brown yelled. His head whipped back toward me.

We went faster. Gravity pulled us along. Our feet barely touched the earth. We ran like a rope was pulling us. Skinny branches ripped at our shins. I kept my eyes open and everything in front of me bled together and made me dizzy, rock-leaf-root-dirt. We came out through the trees. We'd been gone since the morning and now there wasn't much light left. The whole town was waiting for us. They wanted to see who the Marathon Girl was running with.

Race! Race! Race! they yelled. They pumped their fists at the sky. They pumped their fists at the mountain.

No no! we yelled. No thank you! We elbowed away their cups of water. The crumpled cups fell around our feet. Cold water splashed our ankles and got into the toe boxes of our shoes.

What if your feet get rusty? I yelled, but Emanuel didn't hear me. *Click click clickity click clickity click click*, went his metal ankles, faster and faster.

What if we never stop running? I yelled. He brought his knees up and down, higher and higher. We were running past my house.

I live there! I yelled and Emanuel Brown ran up my steps and jumped off my porch. He didn't seem worried about his feet at all.

We ran past all the people and the corner and the gas station with my car still on the lot. We ran past the downtown. There was a sale on macaroni. The sign winked at me from the grocery store window. We were running like two people falling out of a car, our arms and legs travelling at different speeds and in different directions. Emanuel Brown made big circles with his arms as he ran. I hopped up and down and sang to make my heart go slower. I sang *Froggy Went A Courtin'* and a Spanish song about a travelling salesman who carries the world in his bag. I sang until I was out of breath.

On our way out of town, we ran by the tire fire. The two guys in brown overalls put down their shovels and watched us go. I think they were in shock. They didn't even call us sluts.

We ran between the piles of tires and let our arms trail behind us. Sparks landed on our clothes and burned there until they exhausted themselves.

Watch your sleeve, I said to Emanuel and he said, What?

I reached out and grabbed at his hand. The whole hand was warm, even the fingers. His wrist flexed and for a second I could feel all the veins stand out straight, with Emanuel's blood inside them.

We ran until we were on a dirt road with no trees or bushes to slow us down. I couldn't remember ever feeling cold. We ran like a hot gust. If we ran by you, all you would feel was the spray of sand kicking up against your cheekbones. If you were behind us, all you would see was ash.

SUPER CARNICERÍA

They floated into the morning on their backs, back and forth in the cloverleaf outdoor hot tub at the Water Tower Hotel. It was June 16. Anna had her eyes closed and when she squinted up it wasn't night anymore. The sky flipped open. They weren't floating: Aubrey had pulled two deck loungers off the side and set them up in the shallow water so they could lie there in the froth with less risk of drowning.

He was her captain. He took responsibilities seriously. They'd landed at two on a Saturday afternoon—forty-two passengers, one baby, no wheelchairs—but wouldn't be out again until four on the Sunday. The cloverleaf hot tub in Sault Ste. Marie.

The thing about twenty-six hours on the ground is you have to do something. You can't do nothing. They hadn't done a fucking thing in New York, but the potential is there in a big city and the potential fills you up. Northern Ontario, you need something else to do that.

Anna's brother was Zoran. She'd pulled a booklet of photographs out of her wallet the night before, hand-stapled and ordinary. Primary colours for background.

Zoran, black-haired and with a cockeyed look, mouth open as though speaking to the camera, his grade one school picture. Happy-looking, but not smiling.

Loud-looking.

What do you mean? Anna said.

Looks like one of those kids who never shuts up, Aubrey said.

One photo a year for ten years. He always wore a red shirt for picture day. He couldn't wear a collar, or shirts with tags. He couldn't wear shoes without socks. If he didn't wear socks he'd spend all day yelling about his feet, how bad they felt with no socks on them.

Sort of a retard? Aubrey said, but kindly. He meant no harm. A loud retard he could understand.

Sort of, Anna said, lying back on the hotel carpet. They were in his room, waiting for another flight crew to get in from the airport so the night could start up for real. The ceiling stucco-painted white, the curtains brown, the bedding burgundy, the carpet dry-feeling on the backs of her arms and neck. The kind of carpet that's just for show: easy-clean, sanitized to prickling.

He was missing an enzyme, she said, and swooshed her arms and legs together and apart, together and apart. Making a carpet angel.

What's that? Aubrey said, dropping to the floor with a bottle in one hand. He had a couple of cheap glasses from the bathroom, plastic-wrapped against dirt, and he tried to get his thumbs inside the plastic to break it off.

Pretty strong wrap. The wrangling just cracked the cups and Aubrey smiling like Fuck you motherfucker.

This was Anna's first layover since the funeral.

They could have watched the Sault Aurora but instead they got drunk. They drank cheap beers and ate chicken and baked potatoes without sour cream but with salt and so much pepper the skins crackled in their teeth. In the Husky restaurant, ten minutes down the road from the hotel. After dinner she'd wanted to find the other crew but back in his room Aubrey pulled the forty of vodka out of a dresser drawer.

The second crew came in at nine. Anna lay down and made the angels until they showed up, her bare arms raw against the blue carpet. Aubrey and Anna, and then the Captain and First Officer and Purser plus two more girls off the other pairing. Anna's girl Jeannie also sitting in the room but not drinking, polishing her nails on the bed.

Where's your FO all this time? The other captain was Karol. Or Pavel. She wasn't listening.

Pavel lined up two sets of disposable plastic drinking cups. He had long fingers with long bones in them. He slit the plastic wrap and skinned the cups like a hunter.

Beating off to porn, Aubrey said. What the fuck do I know?

Between the seven of them they drank the vodka in little waves. They took a cab down to the Docks and thought about shooting pool but didn't and went back to drinking beer. The girls all sitting in a row on the high bank and three pitchers between them on tall bar tables. The other Purser was new, or new enough that Anna had never flown with her before, never even seen her in the crew lounge: black hair and eyes and the faintest, delicate-bleached moustache. She turned to Anna.

I'm not even supposed to be here, she said. I'm supposed to be at home. I just got back from vacation, and Harold calls me in at four in the morning. I haven't been home! I just sat on my bed and cried.

Where you went on vacation? Pavel said.

Curaçao. Oh my God, you have to go. Wait. Look at these. She reached down and dug into her purse for her phone.

Aubrey leaned across the table and pushed a pint of amber at Anna. Emergency situation, he said.

Anna: I know this one. There's a couple fornicating in the lav, and you've already called Cabin Secure. What do you do?

You're using that one tomorrow. There's your brief.

Sober Jeannie laughing with all her blonde hair, her feet and shoes tucked up under her on the bench. Pregnant, Anna happened to know, but not showing yet and this was important since she'd taken off her ring sometime between the hotel and the bar. Anna looked at the curve of Jeannie's legs on the high bench, her tiny feet in their black shoes. No belly yet, not even if you squinted.

You'd call the guys, right? Jeannie said.

What?

About the couple in the lav. That's what you'd do, right? Call the guys? And then you'd have to do your Secure all over again.

See? Aubrey said. It's a real situation. It could happen.

Yeah, I'd call you and tell you all about it, Anna said. Real slow.

Pavel bought a round of shots, and then another. Then a free round from the bartender.

My friend! Pavel said, when the girl brought the newest round on a tray.

The black-haired Purser now happy to be out. She swirled the shot glass in one hand and watched the liquid spin, then put it back quick and returned to her vacation slideshow.

Okay, so this was the beach restaurant, right?

Her thumb scrolling down the screen. You have to see this lobster we ate. They put a little hat on him.

Jeannie sipped from a lowball glass of ginger and lime bar mix, pushed her shot glass at Anna when no one was looking.

Listen, Anna said. You won't get fired if you tell. She leaned over and poured the shot into Pavel's beer. They give you this little maternity uniform. And you don't have to wear heels! Shelagh Manus had a baby flying six-leggers. She flew till eight months.

Jeannie reached over and squeezed her fingernails into Anna's wrist. It won't be the same, she hissed. You know it won't.

Anna slumped against Jeannie for a moment, like sisters.

Where's your ring?

Jeannie caressed her own hand.

Sometimes I dance with them a little, she said.

The guys?

I don't think there's anything wrong with it.

Would you do it if he was here? Anna sat up and pointed to an empty spot on the bench. Pretend he was here, in the room.

Pretend is pretend, Jeannie said.

Anna knew when she'd got in the cab with the rest of them that she'd be stuck and then drunk and the next day on the aircraft would hurt. It was a thing she did on purpose. Spring and summer being high times for rough air; all those hot pockets rising. What Pavel's crew had going for them was an eight a.m. wheels-up. This, if nothing else, promotes moderation. Aubrey and Anna the last to leave the bar.

Lights on?

Another cab ride home?

They woke up in the cloverleaf tub and there was the sun and they said goodnight. She couldn't remember if she'd kissed him the night before or what.

Did I kiss you? At the bar?

You showed me your brother.

Anna remembered then: her hand in her coat pocket, thumbing the little booklet.

All the pictures?

The top one. You said he got scars later.

Her blue trench and the little black shoes lying poolside. O-ho.

Before anything, before crawling onto his bed, before sleep, she double checks all her pockets, both hands at once, down and through and up and out, and then turns them inside out, and throws the purse upside down, but the photos are gone. Empty. Swept into a corner at the bar or face down in a puddle or caught in the pool filter or wedged into the seat of the taxi, but not here, not in her pocket, not on the floor.

You'd find the booklet and think, Some mother's collection. You'd look around for the wallet it came out of, lost money or lottery tickets or a credit card maybe not even cancelled yet. All this before flipping the little pages. Zoran through the years. One enzyme, absent. In the top picture Zoran is still clean and intact.

Then a disease that builds up over time. Too much uric acid in the blood, gets into all your organs. Kidney problems: hips and elbows and knuckles swollen with gout. Moderate retardation, low muscle tone. No motor control. Frustrating. So frustrating that by late childhood you might bang your head off the wall, you might gnaw at your own tongue and lips, then later your fingers, starting from the nail and working in to the first knuckle, then the second. All the fine parts that won't work.

This is how Anna explains it, lying on Aubrey's bed and staring straight up.

He chewed his lips off? Aubrey tucks her in, pins her by the shoulders: You have to sleep now. We're out in four hours.

He picks up her hand and sucks on two of her fingers a moment, pretend-chewing them, then pulls them out and holds them in the air.

I think we got no problems with these ones, he says.

Anna laughing. Who's gonna find those pictures? Then: Put your hand over my mouth, cover my mouth. Aubrey, cover my mouth.

He does. He lets her scream. His hand gets wet: the breath steams out of her. She screams until the voice coming out is cracked and thin and when Aubrey takes his hands off her face she still wants him on her. She holds his wrists. They're sober but remember being drunk.

When he's done she wants to trade places, and she leans up over him and holds him down with her hands under his collarbone. She's still wearing a t-shirt. She puts one hand over his mouth.

He chewed his own lips off, she says, rocking him back and forth. And his fingers. He had no finger-tops, no nails, he went down to the knuckle.

He could have done anything, she says. Any crime, they couldn't catch him.

Aubrey catches his breath.

You get it? she says. He had no fingerprints.

At the airport, the power's out and it's hailing and an old man smiles while Anna counts change for the vending machine.

Other stewardesses go to Rome, Paris, London, he says. You get to overnight in Sault Ste Marie.

New York yesterday, she says. And Chicago tonight. So I guess I'm okay.

The man's smile sags a little. He's tired of her already.

She doesn't want this old man here. She wants Aubrey standing next to her, close enough that if she fell his body might stop the falling. She wants the right change for a bottle of juice. She looks around. Aubrey is up at the ticket counter, leafing through the pack of flight plans. She can see his lips moving as he reads. Alternate: Sudbury. Flight level Two-Three-Oh. Expected passengers: Fifty-three.

Someone takes a step toward her and Anna jumps back.

Listen you blonde bitch, the old man whispers. His eyes are a watery grey.

No. He doesn't say a thing. His body hasn't moved. He's timid and disappointed. The girls always seem so nice when they're up in the air. Why is this one so mean?

Hope you got some hot coffee on that airplane for me, he says.

She presses a hand on the juice button.

You like the way we take care of you, yeah? she tells the old guy. Bring you tea and cookies when your seatbelt is on. Maybe you wanna sit in my lap?

The plastic bottle of juice smacks down into the bottom of the machine.

Aubrey catches this from where he's standing in his hat and long coat. She looks up and realizes he's been watching for some time. He takes a warning step toward them. Shakes his head, then points to the ladies' room. He's her only witness: Jeannie and the First Officer in the back room with egg sandwiches, eating off napkins with the draft blowing through the gap in the door to the ramp.

Anna cracks the seal of her grapefruit juice and drinks it on the toilet in the dark airport, slipping a couple Advil down alongside. When it's time to go, Aubrey walks into the Ladies' and rattles the cubicle door. She comes out and wipes her mouth with the back of her hand.

Can't go flying without you, Aubrey says.

He tows her little suitcase. At security bypass he watches as she pulls off her glove, presses her fingertip into the scanner long and deep and slow.

She was seven when Zoran was born. Small and purple in her mother's bed, little fists curling around the edge of the eiderdown and for eight weeks he screamed.

Anna carried him up and down. Once she carried him by his feet and gave him a shake, to stop the screaming, but her mother took him away. Her mother waiting for him to do the normal things: sit up at six months, crawl, get on his feet and rock against the living room coffee table. He didn't babble. He vomited. They had to abandon a red couch when they moved apartments because there was so much baby vomit plastered down behind the cushions and who wants to sit on that?

A bit slow, the doctor thought, Maybe the mother a bit old for new babies.

He peed orange.

He learned to talk but it sounded wrong. He spat. When he walked his legs kicked out funny. He fell down. He had trouble eating. He couldn't get his hand to the right place, into his mouth. His hand with food in it. The mother put on music and he danced with his whole body, arms and legs spastic with joy.

When he was three and she was ten Anna fell asleep every night to the sound of his head, banging off the wall between their rooms. Rigorous.

Your colleague doesn't like me.

This is Anna's old man again, the man from the airport. They're standing back in the galley of the plane, Anna sorting dirty napkins from empty beer cans for recycling, Jeannie dropping used glasses into a tray.

Jeannie looks up: The lavatory is at the front of the cabin, sir.

The man looks confused, turns, and heads up to the front of the plane where a handful of people are standing, hunched, waiting in turn for the bathroom door to open.

How many times a day do I say that? Jeannie says. She slides the glass tray back into its compartment, latches the door, pulls out an empty metal canister and sits down on it.

You should have told him I'm your managing flight attendant. Anna hasn't moved. She's poised over the garbage bag, arms raised, two empty cans of Molson Canadian in each hand. I'm the Purser on this flight, she says. We provide consistent service to all passengers.

Jeannie looks up. He wanted the lav. Right? He was asking for the lav?

There's a pause. Anna's not sure now. What was the man talking about?

Where did you fly before?

I used to bartend, Anna says. And I was a nanny for these two little girls.

That's the same job as this, Jeannie says. She's filling out bar paperwork on her lap: how many bottles did you start with, how many did you use.

I flew with Sky for seven years, and then charters with Soleil for a year and a half, Jeannie says. Our passengers are so chill compared to that. You fly vacation charters, people are throwing food at you. But you get the layovers, so.

Anna pulls out a cart and steps on the brake, locking the wheels while she sets up her bar top. She reaches up and pulls down a coffee pot, looks it over. Unscrews the lid and goes to throw the switch on a hot jug to fill the pot with coffee.

Jeannie stands up.

No one's drinking coffee at this time, she says. Don't bother. Here. She takes the pot out of Anna's hands and latches it back in its compartment. Just put lots of water, beer, two whites and a red.

Jeannie unlocks the brake, pushes the cart at Anna.

I'll go first, you can follow me. If someone wants coffee, I'll get you to run for it. Okay? She pulls out her own cart and cuts the brake with her shoe. A bell rings: woman at row 6.

Don't worry that you didn't fly before, Jeannie says. This whole place is just daycare with drinks.

She backs into the aisle, towing her bar cart behind her.

Get people on a plane, she says, suddenly everyone's in Pampers.

There's no one in the last row, so after they're done service Anna slides into a passenger seat and pushes up on the white plastic shade. The blue outside hurts her head and she almost pulls it down again, but natural light is good for you, helps you sleep at night. Out the window it's bright and sinister. The plane drops and starts. Jeannie already has a seatbelt tight around her belly. A rough patch of air; *une zone de turbulence*.

She gets her phone out, hops up out of her seat and refastens next to Anna.

Okay look, she says. I'm fourteen weeks, so that's right here.

I don't know what this is, Anna says.

It's Baby Bump Pro, Jeannie says. It's an app. It tells you where the baby's at every week.

Anna cups a hand around the screen. There's still some glare off the window but she can make out a drawing of a fetus, its skin transparent, weird legs curled up. All the ribs showing, skinny. Half the thing is just a head, eyes closed and lids blue with blood vessels. *By now your baby is about 3 inches long*, she reads, *and weighs nearly an ounce. Her tiny, unique fingerprints are now in place.*

Do you know what you're having? Anna says.

I only had sisters, Jeannie says. So I don't know what you say to a boy. She flips ahead to eighteen weeks, then twenty, then twenty-eight. The legs get longer; the skin is still see-through.

Jeannie swipes a finger across the screen and the image changes and she tosses the phone back in her purse.

God, she says. Boys. What would you even say?

There's a giant man on top of the optician's, holding a sign that says Eye Can See You Now. They're in the shuttle, down from the airport to the hotel. Everything is enormous in Chicago. A giant bull on top of the steakhouse, a white plaster horse outside Tony's Western Wear, and then the fast stream of carbon copy taco shops. Taquería, Quesadillas, Gorditas.

Jeannie: A Gordita is like a Taco Bell thing, right?

Gordita, it means like, little fat one. It means, something that fattens you up, Anna says. A fattener. In a good way.

Jeannie shifts straighter and sucks in her gut. Day three of four days out, seventeen hours now on the ground at Midway. Light loads for weekend flying.

How fat do you think you'll get, Anna whispers. Thirty pounds? Fifty pounds?

Jeannie picks her nose, lightly, in the window. The guys are sitting up front and don't see. Anna sees. She smoothes the lapel on her trench coat, adjusts the flight report envelope where it's sticking a little too far out of her purse.

Where's your hat? she says.

Jeannie turns: In my lunch bag.

In the room, Anna unzips her case and lets it spill open on the floor. Aubrey hangs his coat in her closet, next to the ironing board. She pries off her high heels and throws them at his feet.

I'll just stay, he says. He's got a key she handed him at the desk, for a room down the hall, and he slips it into the coat pocket and starts peeling off his uniform, hanging up each piece: jacket, then tie, then shirt.

She takes the running shoes out of her bag, and a pair of shorts and some socks and gets up and goes into the bathroom to change. There's a click from the little doorknob lock, and she unlocks it and then clicks it again, just to be sure.

Kicker Blvd. Or Knicker. Kiefer. Turn left here.

No: Kedzie.

She's the only runner in this part of Chicago, every sidewalk a construction project, every corner broken down and pyloned-off and a quick jump down into the road. If you run in the Sault, you go along the shoulder with the airfield on one side of you and forest on the other. They warn you about coyotes. A few years ago a girl got eaten. Not right there, but in the province, and now they're seeing coyotes near the airport all the time so it stands to reason.

Here at Midway you go along the north side of the park until the houses start to break down and then at the light you turn up.

You don't run all the way to Englewood, not if you're white, not if you're a lady, not if you're wearing anything that can be stolen. On 63rd there's no houses, no park, just signs and signs and signs: Lavandería, Secadora. 7 Día Adventencia Filadelfia, two hands gripping each other in friendship, hands with no bodies attached. On the seventh day we painted these shaking hands; these hands, shaking.

Super Carnicería. The butcher's sign hand-painted: a cha-cha of laughing, well-fed pigs and advancing, dancing cleavers. American pomp and broken-down Mexican joints. Valentina's. Los Poncho's. Mis Tacos.

How many Mis Tacos you make, lady?

Anna speeds up, her stride shortens. On West Marquette there's a low-rise and a one-armed black man outside it with his dachshund. The dog gets up and goes for her a little.

Cheeto! This is the one-arm, booming. Get back here!

The man is fat. He's probably younger than Anna but lives harder. He's wearing Adidas pants and a t-shirt, with nothing coming out the sleeve of the t-shirt on the west side; so, his right arm.

How often does a one-arm man get laid?

How do you lose an arm in the twenty-first century?

A soldier, right? Home now in Bedford Park with his dog,

standing out on the broken sidewalk and looking across at Marquette. Was left- or right-handed before. Blocks away, Anna thinks about slipping a hand up his empty sleeve, the feeling of the stump. It's not too late to turn around. She wants it raw and textured, but can't imagine anything that's not the sealed, plastic feel of a bent knee. The joint, coated. This fat man in her bed.

At a boarded-up store Anna sees the hollow between broken glass and plywood and thinks Who lives there? Lures her black man through, fucks him a moment in the debris, her mouth on the stump, his stomach hard and bloating against her.

Blinks him away.

She used to read to him. At his school the doctor told them Zoran was as smart as a normal boy, but he couldn't do normal things. All the smartness was caught, folded up inside his brain, and what came out was torture. He could swear. He said No to things he wanted. He said the opposite.

She scooted him down the marble hallways in his wheelchair.

If she got him alone he yelled, Let's be international! and she yelled back, Shall we travel the world and sleep in tents?

No! We'll sleep in grand hotels!

Will our fame precede us?

The doctor said the biting was not as simple as self-injury.

By the time he was eight, most of his lower lip missing, a piece of the inside of his cheek, a chunk gone from his tongue. When he started on his fingers, they strapped his arms to the arms of the chair. They locked the chair brakes on and it lurched with his impulse to get hand to mouth.

They do things they don't want to do, the doctor said.

We're here to help.

Whenever Anna came to visit, Zoran wore a red shirt with no collar.

X-linked.

Anna tells this to Aubrey, later, in bed, her sweaty clothes and wet towel bunched up in the armchair where he was sitting when she got back to the room.

It means a girl can't get it. But my mother had it on her gene.

He's got his fingers in her hair, tangled still from the shower, picking through the damp knots.

I can't have babies, she says. I'm never doing that.

Jeannie rubs her belly in the back of the shuttle. They're stopped at the light at W 65th. They've got a 6:40 report and a 7:55 wheels-up. Aubrey taps a hand off Anna's knee like it's his own knee.

The hand wants the light to change, the shuttle to move, the wheels to roll.

A little kid gets out of a car and crosses the street, heading for McDonald's. It's wearing a denim jacket and has long, curly hair. It's carrying a doll's umbrella. The mother is regular-size, towers over the kid. They don't hold hands.

That's the smallest fucking midget I ever saw, Aubrey says. They've turned their bodies to the back window now. His hand goes still and heavy on her leg. The walking baby is like a magnet to them.

Jeannie says, Primordial dwarfism.

She looks at Anna and Aubrey like, What?

I used to babysit this kid and now he has a kid that has it, she says, that's the only reason why I know.

She flips her back against the seat and pulls something out of the pocket of her trench. A little book. She plays her thumb against the edge and lets the pages ripple.

What you got there. Aubrey leans forward, his arm across Anna's body as though the van might throw her forward.

I don't know, Jeannie says. I found it in the bar, when we were in the Sault. It's kind of demented. It's kind of gross. It's like this kid was normal and then someone just cut him and cut him. People are sick.

She tosses the photos onto the seat beside her, then picks them up again and turns the booklet over in her fingers. Aubrey looks at Anna.

Anna just looks out the window.

It's not real, she says. You'd get arrested. It's just a promo for some movie, some whatever, indie-Sault low-budget horror movie.

Jeannie shrugs, slides the book back in her pocket.

The shuttle heaves forward with the green light. Outside the dwarf walks into McDonald's. Where it will order what?

Anna turns to Aubrey.

A Happy Meal, she says. Half-a-Happy-Meal. Half-a-half-a-Happy-Meal.

You have a happy meal, he says. He's got yesterday's flight plans out of their envelope and keeps his eyes down on the weather map.

Jeannie reads the street names off their signs and calls them out loud. South Kolin, South Kenneth, South Kilbourn. She's a pretty-girl-getting-older, blue eyes, the kind of straight hair you only get with an iron. A little bulge under her uniform, barely noticeable. You'd never notice. Soft arms, small feet, fingernails painted creamy white.

And her pink glossed mouth, South Cicero South Cicero

South Cicero.

    I think you're showing, Anna says.

    She says, I can see your baby's head.

    Jeannie stops then, her lips soft and gaping.

    The kind of mouth you can really get your teeth into.

JIM AND NADINE,
NADINE AND JIM

They were watching the earthquake news and she jumped up out of her chair.

Don't start! Jim said. Don't start!

I can't watch! Nadine said. The orphanage! They need help! Her brown hair was short and ragged next to her face and she hopped up and down from one foot to the other to keep herself from running away.

Stand still! Jim said. He sank his hand into the bowl of cheezies and crunched his fist closed. The hand was orange with cheezie dust right up to the wrist.

Nadine stepped onto a nearby beanbag cushion and stood absolutely still.

I'm fine, she said from her cushion. Don't worry, Jim, I'm fine, I'm fine.

On the television, babies were stacked on bakers' racks because there were no more mattresses. Their little blankets were damp and streaked with grime, but overall the babies did not look any more unhappy than regular babies. They were tucked in close on the shelves. The orphanage had been knocked down by the earthquake.

Smashed flat, Nadine said, and she punched herself in

the chest—a double-fist punch.

You're all mixed up! Jim said. You don't know what's going on! Rest and relax, rest and relax, that's what I always say! He leaned forward in his armchair, elbows on knees, hands out flat. There wasn't much meat on him. He was a tall enough guy with big hands.

It's my heart! Nadine said. She coiled down onto the cushion like a little warm bun.

Chrissakes, Jim said, his flat hands wavering back toward the cheezie bowl. Run a tub.

Nadine scooped her knees into her chin and held onto her ankles.

Don't cry! Jim said. You know how that upsets me! His mouth was all orange. Don't cry, do your grounding! Jesus, feel your feet!

In moments of panic Nadine had been taught to stand up and feel the pressure of her whole body bearing down through her calves and feet. This was called grounding. She was meant to feel grounded as opposed to, Nadine thought, airborne. Nadine found more comfort in an airborne self, a self that could float up and away from frightening things, but the therapist said No, Nadine needed to push all the fear out through her toes.

I'm turning off the TV, Jim said, but he didn't. On the screen, a white doctor was talking about all the legs he'd cut off since the earthquake. If a person's leg was caught under a rock or a piece of broken concrete, it was the doctor's job to cut off the leg, and there wasn't any anaesthetic because the wrong boats had got to the island first.

Aren't you traumatized? the reporter asked and the doctor said, Yes, yes the screaming was very hard to ignore.

He doesn't even look like a doctor, Jim said. Where's

his coat?

Nadine pulled up and fixed her feet flat on the ground.

I feel my feet, Nadine said. She was already crying.

Nadine flattened both hands over her mouth to hold the crying down. I feel my feet, she said into the hands.

Just don't look! Jim said. Look out the window. He took off his t-shirt and tied it in a big knot, pulling tight on the two ends, and he walked up the stairs like that, tearing at the ends of the shirt. When he got to the bedroom, he stood under the doorjamb and bounced on the balls of his feet. Nadine! he yelled down the stairs. Are you still crying?

Nadine pressed her fingers harder against her mouth until she could feel her teeth, flat and even, on the other side.

Out the window, the school bus stopped and all its flashing lights were on. Cars lined up behind. A little girl with dark hair and a blue backpack stepped off the bus and crossed the street in front of it. The girl was only about as tall as the bus tires, but the driver saw her, so it was okay. He didn't run over the girl. No other cars squashed the girl, either. On the other sidewalk, there was a woman with long hair and a little dog on a green leash waiting for her.

On the television, three men were beating a fourth man for stealing a bag of corn.

What if I stay upset forever? Nadine said to her hands. She used her imagination to build a wall in the hallway, halfway between her body and the bedroom. She laid the wall brick by brick and licked the mortar off her finger. It was white and coarse, like the rock dust on the people's legs on television.

Nadine sat down on the couch and picked up the remote and shut off the TV. She pulled her knees up tight to her chest and rubbed her shins. The bumpiness of the shin bone always made Nadine think of her spine. The shin = the spine of the leg. She rubbed downwards, so any leftover fear would know what direction it ought to travel.

That brick wall calmed her right down.

Jim came pounding down the hall wearing his jacket.

It's supposed to be me that makes you feel better, he said. His keys jingled in his coat pocket where his hand was shaking them around. Why won't you let me make you better?

He stood with his thighs against the arm of the couch. Nadine looked at the waistband of his jeans, slumping low over his hipbone. The hip looked like a horn. Jim held out his big hand and Nadine let him wrap it around her small one. She thought about the bricks in her wall. Their crumbling weight, the sharp edges and grainy mortar. It didn't matter now about the earthquake because at least Jim wasn't mad. She leaned her cheek against his hip.

Jim said, Nadine! What if you stay upset forever?

Jim had not always been Nadine's boyfriend. He had first, and for a period of some months, been the boyfriend of Nadine's sister, until the sister decided to hone her skills as a shell game practitioner. She moved to the coast based on the quite reasonable assumption that it would be easier to acquire shells in an oceanic environment. Now of no fixed address, she housesat on houseboats when the owners came ashore for bungalow vacations, and lived very well like this with a new boyfriend and a trained black parrot named Hollister.

Jim first met Nadine at Christmas, the family dinner.

Nadine is *sen-si-tive*, the sister had whispered across the table to where Jim sat. Nadine, next to him, wearing a crown made of red tissue paper, had flashed him her tiny teeth.

Jim patted Nadine's shoulder and then her knee and, later on, when the sister stepped out for some soothing ginger ale, he patted most of the rest of her body as well. It was a good arrangement and suited them fine, and when the sister climbed into her car and pointed west, it only made sense for Jim to come and live at Nadine's house full time.

Nadine offered him her keys and Jim put them in his pocket.

Now Nadine showed Jim that she was not upset forever. She did this by smoothing his eyebrow hairs until they were silky and stray-free as little eye-toupées. Jim took her panties off and they settled in. He jumped forward a little with his hips and every time he did she gave a little equal-and-opposing jump. She bit his beard. Things went on like this for some time. She wrapped her arms around him and pushed her fingers against his tailbone, the boniest place on his whole bony body, and pressed down, holding him inside her.

Nadine thought about how Jim tasted. How he tasted all the same—his mouth and tongue were no different than his cum. His shoulders slammed downward and she thought, Your inside parts taste the same as your outside parts. I will never get tired of fucking you. But then after a few minutes she went back to repeating words in her own head. She bites his beard, she bites his beard, she thought to herself. She was too tired to come, anyway. The earthquake had exhausted her. Jim pulled out and wiped some blood off his dick and Nadine said, Oh would you look at that, then swung her legs onto the floor and went to mark the calendar.

They went to the pub for dinner. Nadine turned the newspaper over so that the front cover lay flat against the table. Whatever the cover has to show, Nadine said, the table can look at it. She liked to read the horoscope and the Ann Landers reprints. On her way to the bathroom the bartender smiled at her. He had brown eyes and was eating curry chips. Nadine could smell the curry. His mouth curved and he licked the gravy from his thumb.

Sometimes, if Jim was sleeping and wouldn't notice she was gone, Nadine came in and had a pint on her own. Once she had sat at the bar and cried over the crossword because she'd done it all in pen and it was wrong and needed fixing, and the brown-eyed bartender had brought her a slice of pie. You're just a wee little thing, he said. And you push yourself awfully hard.

Now Nadine walked right by him, because Jim was there of course, but she raised her own thumb to her sweet, tiny teeth and bit down. She went into the bathroom and sat for a moment, and then she wiped her bum and washed her hands and walked back to the table. Jim was eating a burger and Nadine had chicken fingers. She picked up a slice of lemon and squeezed the juice all over her meat.

If you don't start paying attention to me, Jim said, I'm going to have to start seeing other women on the side.

That Suzanne Grady, he said. She's always trying to sit in my lap.

Nadine looked over at Suzanne, who was their waitress. Suzanne was leaned up against the bar, twirling a string of blonde hair around one finger and staring at the teletype news on a screen mounted over her head. There was a piece of banana meringue pie on the bar in front of her and the bartender was eating it and reading the sports. He lifted the meringue layer off with his fork and the banana custard went down in two bites.

I gave you a blowjob last night, Nadine said. A long one. What are you talking about?

Yeah, a blowjob, Jim said. But was it sincere?

Nadine said she wasn't sure how a blowjob could be more sincere.

I think you've given better blowjobs in the past, to other guys you knew before you knew me, Jim said. I get all your leftover blowjobs. What's wrong with you, anyway?

You are throwing the baby out with the bath water, here, Jim. Nadine crunched a carrot stick and it was very angry crunching. You can have Suzanne if you want her. She looks like a horse, Nadine said. Ridden hard and put away wet.

Then Jim pushed up to leave and Nadine had to beg him on her knees to stay because she had left her wallet at home. She didn't even have her wallet and who was going to pay for all these chicken fingers and burgers?

Across the room, the brown-eyed bartender looked up, his fork quivering with meringue.

One lousy burger, Jim said. But he went with Nadine to the bar and paid, because she was really on the verge of being upset and she might stay upset forever and then what would he do? Suzanne Grady took the money and made change with her belt. Her hands took the cash and went into the pockets on the belt and came out again with coins. She was able to do all of this without taking her eyes off the teletype.

Jim put the coins down on the bar. Nadine noticed that the bartender had left a sliver of meringue and that he had folded up the sports. The bartender kept his eyes on Jim but his sugary plate moved slyly along the bar toward Nadine. Her finger inched toward the leftover pie. Jim turned to go and she popped the meringue in her mouth. Where it exploded and melted away, all at once.

They walked up the hill to home.

You're a fucking cow, that's you, Jim said. You're an ice-heart bitch.

I don't even know what I've done wrong, Nadine said. We were eating lunch, she said. She wished he'd left her at the bar. She wished he'd left her there in some way that was not her fault.

Jim tore at a hangnail with his teeth and spat it onto the sidewalk. When he walked uphill, his arms hung funny, loose and long like an ape's—a thing Nadine always noticed but didn't bother saying out loud.

Another thing: he said "foil-age" instead of "fol-iage." She had a secret list.

It was warm out and an old lady in her front yard stopped pulling weeds to watch them go by, Nadine taking three steps to each one of Jim's.

When they got up to the house, he took the stairs two at a time and threw himself against the bed, flipped open his computer and said, Go away. I don't love you anymore.

Jim looked at his computer screen. Nadine looked at Jim. Just remember you're the one who said it, Nadine told him, and then that was that. She ran down the stairs, but remembered she didn't have her car keys and dragged herself back up to the bedroom again.

Jim was standing in the closet, tearing her French Maid costume into pieces. He looked up. You'll have to get something new for the next guy!

His eyebrows were messy, as though he had been taking a long nap. In fact, the opposite was true, Nadine thought. His eyebrows were working entirely too hard.

She left the house walking. There were tulips everywhere, beginning to fade: the petals were limp and looked burnt along their edges. The sagging petals were like wobbly limbs, Nadine thought. It was too bad flowers didn't have shins. Those tulips needed backbone.

She came home when it was dark. Jim maybe sleeping.

Sleeping his mood off, Nadine called it. Sometimes he slept for days. She was in the kitchen holding marshmallows over the toaster when she heard a knock, and then another and another. Nadine licked the sugar from her fingers. The knocking wasn't the front door, it was upstairs, like in a scary movie where the phone rings and rings and when you pick it up the operator tells you to get out of the house.

You could make a book of my life, Nadine said to the toaster, and she went up the stairs to where the knocking was.

Nadine, Jim said. It's Jim.

But she couldn't see him. He was still in the bedroom. Nadine tried the knob and it turned, but the door wouldn't open. For a second she stood quiet and still. It did not seem a completely bad thing to find Jim's body on one side of a door, and her own body on the other.

It was true she'd be in trouble if she didn't get him out.

She pushed her thin frame up against the door. She gave it shoulder. Nothing.

The door's stuck, she said.

Jim, on the other side, let drop a few curses. Then: I've nailed it shut, he said.

Where did you get the nails?

For fuck's sake, I been peeing in the garbage can. Can you not knock the thing down?

Nadine: I'm just a wee little thing, Jim.

You're not, you're massive!

I'll call someone to come around and help me?

No!

Well, then, Nadine said. I've seen you put your fist through a wall easily enough. Get yourself out of there. Use a double-fist punch, how 'bout?

Jim said that if he could get an arm through that door and around Nadine's neck, he'd be a happy man, and Nadine imagined just the lanky ape-arm with no Jim attached waving around on her side of the door, covered in rubble and trying to find her throat. I'll just run a tub, then? Nadine said. Rest and relax, Jim, she said. Remember?

Nadine locked herself in the bathroom and opened the window. With both doors shut, bedroom and bathroom, she could still hear him cursing. He would kill them both, he said. Nadine was fucked as a dead horse and half to her grave.

She squirted a heavy dose of dish soap into the tub for bubbles. The night outside her window was warm and black, and she turned the light off in the bathroom too, to see how dark it would get.

She shook her dress down to the floor.

There was the streetlight or the moon. Nadine caught herself in the mirror for just a second and then stayed there a while looking at all her parts: the hard edge of her collarbone, the shoulder, the strict knot of biceps tapering to the eye of her elbow. She firmed up her fist and the biceps tightened. A little more tension and it popped out, round and shadowed. Nadine let the hand drop. She reached for a white towel where they were tucked in close on the shelf. She was surprised at her body, how good it was: small and thin and curved. The bones curved.

A real looker, she was. Banana pie.

Jim was silent now.

Nadine looked down. It was a lovely bath, the bubbles

light as meringue, light as marshmallows resting on the lip of the tub. She touched it with just a toe, then pulled back again. Her knuckles swept the line of her hip.

Out in the night, Nadine imagined the brown-eyed bartender looking up. Her knees locked. Naked and invisible in the black bathroom window, tiny and grounded, just a wee little thing. She reached forward and flipped the switch.

I feel my feet, she whispered to the cool outdoors.

The room swelled with light.

THE ASTONISHING
ABERCROMBIE!

The night she left us my mother packed up some tomato sandwiches for our next-day school lunches and set them in the fridge. She fed the dog. She wiped the counters and the top of the stove—even unplugged the elements and scrubbed around in the drip pan. Nobody ever does that. She arranged the couch cushions the way she liked them best and covered over the piano keys so the cat wouldn't walk on them and disturb our sleep. She did all these things and then she went into the bedroom and packed her one little suitcase, barely enough room for anything in it, locked it tight and walked out the door and walked down the street to the bus stop and waited. When the doors swung open Mama stepped up. I don't know where my father was. Maybe he was downstairs, watching the hockey game. Or out having a beer with Ed Forrester the way he sometimes does. Maybe he came home at one a.m. with a few drinks in him and with lovin' on his mind like that Loretta Lynn song says and found his two boys sleeping and his wife gone. I don't know. In the morning Nana Louise was sitting at the kitchen table and there was a policeman at the counter pouring himself a coffee. The thought that Mama might have willingly left him never occurred to my father. He assumed there had to be foul play involved. Nana Louise had a box of two-ply tissues in front of her and the trash can from under the sink on the floor beside her. She was going through that box at a rate of about two sheets per minute. I figured she had about ten minutes left, tops, if she kept it up. By the looks of the trash can, she'd already been sitting there for an hour easy. That's mathematics at work.

Where's Mama, said Peteyboy, rubbing his eyes.

I hit him good, really knocked his shoulder.

You dumb shit, I said. She's not here. What do you think Nana Louise is here for? Why you think she's crying? I whispered all of this, but real fierce, so he wouldn't go asking any more of his questions.

It's okay, Daddy, I said. She'll come home again, you know she will. I took my father's hand and sat him down next to Nana Louise at the kitchen table. I handed him a Kleenex.

Well, I said, turning to the cop. What do you know, Joe?

The policeman looked at me and he looked at my father. My father just sat there, staring out the window, and let his thumb roll back and forth over the tissue in his hand. The policeman had one of those little notebooks with the coil binding along the top and the pages all messed up. He had a pen too. He made mention of the missing suitcase. He wanted to know, had my mother ever done this before. This disappearing act.

Oh sure, I said. Oh plenty.

I told him how my Mama was a real sensitive soul. A painter. Not like those other mothers you see down the playground, or waiting around at the school bus stop. I pointed to the shabby shack in back of the house where she kept all her canvases and stuff. I showed where we even had one of her paintings hanging up on the living room wall. The officer looked at it for a long time.

Pretty good, he said.

You bet she is! I said. You're not fooling! Why, do you know that my mother painted that whole picture while Peteyboy here was having a nap one afternoon? Start to finish!

I pulled Peteyboy over by his pyjama sleeve. He was like Exhibit A. He was still holding onto his blankie and his bear, and that was just as well because it made him look good and sleepy. You could look at him and really see how Mama might have fit in painting pictures and everything else, all while that boy slept.

You say she's done this before? The policeman looked at my father again, but I know he won't ever tell the truth, so in these situations I like to answer for him.

Yes sir, I said.

My father said, Are you kidding me? Then he yelled it right out loud. Then he said it again low down in his throat and scratched with his thumbnail at a few drops of old milk that had dried onto the table. Nana Louise slapped his hand away. She started scratching the table with her own thumbnail.

The policeman said, What's your name, boy?

I stuck my hand out. A man wants to shake when he's being introduced, don't he?

Abercrombie, I said. But mostly everybody calls me Abe, so I guess you can too.

Well, Abe, when your mother left before—

Which time?

Doesn't matter. What I'm wondering is, do you know where she went?

Now that was a good question. I had to admit, he was

doing his job. Because wouldn't you think, if a woman kept leaving and coming back, coming and going, back and forth, wouldn't you think that she'd have a place she liked to go, like a favourite motel, or even a second family somewhere else. That would make sense, wouldn't it?

No sir, I said. We don't know where she goes. One time she said she'd been to the sea, and she brought us back shells and everything. And the shells had little bits of sand on them that crumbled off and fell into the carpet, so you know she really had been to the sea, and not just to the dollar store. My Nana Louise had to drag the vacuum cleaner up from the basement and paw and paw at the carpet to get the sand out.

When I said this I looked over at Louise. She was using one of her Kleenexes to wipe the gunk out of the corners of the dog's eyes.

Mama says she'd iron all our underwear if we'd let her.

I could see the policeman was waiting on me so I kept on. I said, This other time, she took the bus to the airport and just stayed there a few days, watching the planes taking off and landing and all the people going places and coming home again. And some people who weren't from here were coming here to see what it was like. That time she wasn't gone too long, only a few days, because there's nowhere good to sleep at the airport, just those hard chairs that are all joined together at the arms. And then one time she was gone, oh, a long time, oh, a month at least, and it turned out she hadn't gone hardly nowhere. It turned out she was living in an apartment down Magnolia Street and working as a cashier at the Spare 'n' Save. She liked that cashier work because she said it let her get a real good look at people without them thinking too much of it. She could really look 'em in the eye, she said.

The policeman turned to my father. He kind of took a breath. He said that he didn't think he could see his way clear to filing a missing person report on Mama, because of her history. Because there's a pattern, see: she leaves, then she comes back. Well, shit, that wasn't news to me but you should have seen the snarl come up on my father's mouth.

He stood up and got right in that cop's face.

He said, My wife has been taken in the night. Then he used some very foul language that I won't repeat here, and he used it in a way that was slow and careful and with all his teeth showing.

I tried to make the policeman look at me, instead, so he could see how I was shrugging my shoulders. Normally we don't call the police when Mama leaves. Normally my father just goes to bed until she gets back.

This here's a happy life she's got here! my father said. Just lookit what she's got here!

Nana Louise laughed and laughed. I ripped off a few sheets of paper towel to cover up the spot where the dog was barfing.

Peteyboy had his finger way down in the peanut butter jar. He was having his breakfast.

I could see that the cop looked nervous.

Tell you what, man, he said. If she's not home in three days, you come down to the station and I'll file that report for you. I'll do what I can.

I walked him to the door.

Son, he said. Abe. You've got quite a job ahead of you here, but I can see that you are a quality youngster. I can see that you are up to it and more.

Yeah, I said. I've got a pretty big brain.

We shook hands again and then he got into his squad

car and backed slowly down the driveway and I stood on the porch and waved. When he got to the road he stuck his head out the window and yelled, Betcha she'll be home in time for supper! and I kind of leaned my neck out and looked down the road because I could tell that was what he was expecting and it did make him happy. His mouth opened up nice and wide and I felt good sending him off like that, back to the station with a story to tell and no sad kids at the end of it.

Then I went back inside and told old Nana Louise to go home. I've got a sunny disposition—an optimistic nature, you might say—but watching her sit around and cry was liable to make the other boys, Peteyboy and my father, feel depressed. I told Peteyboy to get his clothes on or we'd be late for school. I fried up some eggs and put the bread on the table and told my father he'd better eat something and then get some sleep. The eggs got all brown and crispy on the bottom which isn't the way I like them, but I had a lot to do and a person can't just stand around watching eggs cook.

How the mornings usually go around here is like this: first me and Peteyboy get up and we wake up Mama. Sometimes she is sleeping in the bed with my father and sometimes she is sleeping on the couch in the living room. You think this is because they are fighting, but it's not. Sometimes one of them or the other has a hard time getting to sleep and then it's easier to toss and turn all by yourself and not in a room where someone else is already sleeping and you feel guilty about it. So wherever she is, we find her and Peteyboy jumps on her but I don't do that anymore because I'm pretty big for that sort of thing. I might sit down in the armchair next to where she's been sleeping and ask her how her night was, and then she'll yawn and roll over and ask me to pass along her robe.

The robe is a really pretty one, long and red and silky with these fancy pictures of birds on it and a tie around the waist. She bought it in Chinatown once when she was visiting New York, back a long time ago before even I was born and maybe before she knew my father. What my mother used to do back then was go to New York and she had enough friends there that she always had someone to stay with and she would live on bread and cheese and when she got sick of that she would live on honey-and-banana sandwiches because it was cheap and at least it wasn't cheese. And she would sit out all day in the park and look at all the sorts of people that came by and if any men tried to talk to her she would always answer in German or Dutch or Italian or something so that they would see she couldn't speak any English and then they'd leave her alone. Some days she would go to the art museums by herself and walk around real slow and try to stand in front of one painting for fifteen minutes before she'd let herself move on to the next one. Some days she'd bring a sketchbook and try to copy some of the paintings, and then some days she'd let herself speak English so that she could find someone to take her to dinner. At night she'd go back to wherever she was staying and she'd have one million stories to tell, or she'd show her book around so her friends could see what she'd been up to all day, and she'd sleep on the couch or on the floor and start all over again the next day.

Even in this little town, at the end of a day she's always got a story about someone she saw and what they said to her and what she said back, so I can imagine how good it was in New York.

So anyway, I pass her along the robe and she wraps herself

all up in it and goes into the kitchen and rolls herself a cigarette, just one. She only does one at a time so that it's not so easy to smoke. Sometimes she lets me lick the paper for her, but sometimes she's in too much of a hurry for that. Then she has a cup of coffee and smokes her cigarette with the window open beside her and looks over any drawings that me and Peteyboy have done lately and she'll run her hand through your hair if she likes the kind of drawing you've done. When she cooks eggs or pancakes or anything, they're always soft with just a little crinkle along the very edge. After me and Peteyboy run and get cleaned up for school she slides into her long coat to cover up the robe, so she can walk us out to the bus stop, but she still wears her high heel slippers because she says it's okay to let those bitches talk.

Only on the mornings Mama's gone, it's me that has to make the eggs because I feel too sorry for my father to make him do any work. He just stands around in his green check pyjama pants and no shirt and when he goes into the bathroom you don't hear that tap-tap noise against the sink that means he's shaving. After we eat, I send him back to bed and make sure that Peteyboy gets cleaned up. Then I go into the bathroom last thing and run a comb through my hair and brush my teeth for real with toothpaste because Mama says only barbarians go around with fuzzy teeth.

Now this is where things get particular. When I went into the bathroom this day I saw something shiny lying next to the sink and it was my mother's gold wedding ring. She must have taken it off to wash her hair before she left, and then forgot to put it back on. Or else maybe she took it off to clean up some mess in the bathroom, some mess that Peteyboy left before he went to sleep. I knew she would want it just as soon as she came back, so I slipped it into the pocket of my jeans for safekeeping. The pocket I put it in was the fifth pocket, you know that really tiny one that sits inside the regular pocket on a pair of Levi's. That's where I put the ring.

If you're wondering did I tell my father or Peteyboy what I found, I did not. I don't know why I didn't. I liked the feel of it, tight and secure in that little pocket and I could reach my finger in and check to make sure it was all right. I could run my fingertip around and around it. It was so smooth. Then I brushed my hair and we went and got on our bikes and rode to school, because if we showed up at the school bus without Mama the other ladies would be asking us questions. It was pretty cold still for biking and my fingers ached when I had to unwind them from the handlebars and get them to do all kind of fancy tricks with the bike locks. But then we were at school, and not much to tell about that. One school is just the same as another, and I guess you've been to school, so you can just imagine.

At lunchtime I was playing a pretty furious game of handball against the side of the building with Tom Kilpatrick and Raji Jones when Geraldine Lafleur came up looking too pleased with herself and stood between us and the wall.

Tom said, Aw, come on, Gerry.

Geraldine is his cousin so he can't talk to her like she's just a regular girl. She's not Raji's cousin, though, and he told her she better move if she didn't want her head whipped off. He had the ball in his hand and he kept trying to fake her out but Geraldine has three brothers and isn't afraid of boys.

She said, You all know Madeleine, don't you? She said it very sweet and high and with a funny smile on. Madeleine Welsher is the new girl, just moved into school about a month before. Most of us have been in the same class since kindergarten. When you get someone fresh, it's big news. So you can see the kind of question it was. Add to that, she's not bad to look at, either. Her hair is really long and curly. It's really happy-looking hair. Her parents moved down from the city and let her wear all sorts of short skirts and thin-strap tops that let her bra show. So I know she wears one.

Well, said Geraldine. Well, Madeleine's father is sponsoring a talent competition for the spring fair. He's putting up the prize—a new bike or two hundred dollars, your choice. I thought I should let you boys know. In case you know anybody with some talent.

Raji let the ball go and it hit Geraldine in the shoulder. The spring fair is a thing that happens at school in April. The choir sings and the recorder group plays and usually the drama group puts on a skit or two. The parents all come and sit on wooden chairs in the gym, and then at the end everybody has to get up and stack their chairs back together so the caretaker can store them away again under the stage in the morning. In short, it's an event for girls. It would be hard to think of a girlier thing to do than be in a spring fair.

Of course there's no arguing that two hundred dollars is a lot of money and I've got just as much talent as the next guy.

Tom said, What kind of bike is it?

A dirt bike, Geraldine said. I want the money if I win.

Madeleine came walking up. I didn't even know she was behind us.

It's a Pithog, she said. 50 cc. Comes with a helmet and gloves and everything. Worth way more than two hundred bucks.

Aw, my mother won't let me ride a dirt bike, Raji said. He went to get his ball that was rolling away. Geraldine rubbed her shoulder. I slipped my finger down into my fifth pocket and felt my mother's smooth ring in there and thought about how happy it would make her to see me winning motocross races on my brand new Pithog that I won by showcasing all my talent. I might even let her paint a picture of me standing next to it. My hair would be all ruffled and I'd have the helmet tucked against my body under one arm and maybe in the other hand I'd be holding a trophy. When I was grown and had made a lot of money racing bikes I could buy her a bigger house with a real fireplace in it, and whenever I went home she'd say, Oh darlin' let me make you a cup of coffee, and we'd sit in the living room and drink our coffee and look up at the picture of me hanging over the fireplace and we'd have a good laugh remembering how I won that bike. It was obvious to me that I was going to have to enter that contest, for Mama's sake of course, and I was just about to say it out loud, too, but then my brother's friend Lucas Pickersgill came running up and said that Peteyboy had biked home after lunch and wasn't back yet and was he in trouble. So instead I went to the principal's office and told them I needed to go home and check on my poor father who was in bed with a fever and had no one to look after him and they told me to be back by two o'clock.

What Peteyboy likes to do when Mama is gone is get up into a tree and watch down the road to see is she coming back yet. You can't fault him for this because he's young and little kids do a lot of worrying. So when I got home that's where he was, with his bike lying on the ground like he had leaned it up against the tree but maybe the tree kicked it away. I dropped my bike into the grass and climbed up onto his branch. At first we didn't say anything, but we just sat there with our thoughts. Peteyboy had Mama's old tape recorder in his lap and some big muffy headphones on his ears. I could tell he wasn't listening to anything because the little wheels inside the tape recorder weren't moving. He just likes to have things over his ears.

It was nice and quiet up there in the tree, with no horns honking or other street-type noises to bother us, and I got to thinking about my Grandpère who was Mama's grandfather before he died and who used to live down the road from us when we still had our old house. He lived there with Grandmère. Even after she passed on, you could tell it was her house. I mean there was the usual old lady stuff like plates hanging on the wall that you don't eat off of, but besides that. What she is like is the lady in the portrait that you see in cartoons, you know? Like when there's a portrait on the wall in some old creepy mansion and some teenagers are exploring the house and they split up and you see the eyes in the portrait following them down the hall. That's what her house was like, only without the portrait. Just the eyes.

Grandpère liked to keep in contact with her when he could. He learned all about a thing called EVP, electronic voice phenomenon, and how even Thomas Edison thought he'd invented a machine that could record voices from the next world. He set up a cassette recorder on the dining room table and every night before he went to bed he hit *record*, and then in the morning he would listen and see what he got. A few of the tapes were duds. But he found some little thing on most of them, either a *hello* or a *darlin'* or a *just fine* and then he labeled them and filed them in a shoe box and stacked all the shoeboxes in his closet. After he died, Mama brought all the shoeboxes home to our house because she said even if the old man was crazy as shit, how could you throw that stuff away? So there they are, stacked up in the shabby shack with all Mama's other stuff. Ghost tapes.

Sometimes Mama pulls out a tape and puts it on when she's working, so you come into the shack and there she is with her big man's shirt on over her clothes, just painting and listening to silence.

Then Peteyboy interrupted these thoughts and said, Remember when Daddy was going to build us a house up in this tree?

Yeah.

You think we could still do that one day?

What, me and you?

Yeah.

I thought about that. We'd need some wood, I said. We'd need some big boards. If we had the right kind of wood, we could do it.

He took off the headphones.

Would we need a ladder?

I said, A ladder would be nice. A ladder would give our house some class.

That's just what I was thinking, too, Peteyboy said. Then he said, Abe?

You ready to go?

Abe?

Yeah.

When I'm trying to go to sleep tonight, will you sing me a song?

I can sing.

But don't tell none of my friends I asked you.

Okay.

Don't tell none of your friends, neither.

Okay.

Okay.

Can we go back to school?

I wanted to talk to him about the EVP to see if he remembered about it too, but he looked so sad and a little like an animal there with the big earphones in his lap that I didn't think talking about ghosts would help him out any. I had to get him down out of the tree. He sounds kind of miserable, but you've got to remember that he's only seven and it's not that easy an age.

It's true what Peteyboy said about the treehouse. Don't ask me how he remembered about it, though. I don't have all the answers. It's like he had some miracle brainwave, because the last time my father talked about it I was maybe six years old, and that makes Peteyboy only two or three.

The way it went was like this: Mama was chiding him about it. She's a tease. She said, Well boys I can see I had better nail a cardboard box up in that tree for you because that's a better house than you'll get from your old man. We were sitting out and eating peanut butter sandwiches for supper at the picnic table and she really had a big cardboard box, too, because the man had come from the furniture store that day and brought her a new washing machine that wasn't so rusty. And Mama said that and Daddy put down his sandwich and went inside the house and slammed the screen door and one of the hinges slapped off, so then the door hung crooked.

I know that was the last time, because I remember that same night Mama and Daddy had a big fight, and they never fight too much, so it's a thing you retain. I don't know what he was so mad about. Mama had just got back from one of her trips, you'd think he'd be glad to see her, and they were yelling and screaming at each other in the hallway and Peteyboy got out of bed and started to cry. He was just standing there in the doorway with his diaper sagging off him and his face all wet and his mouth wide open. Mama went to get him but my father was faster and got him up into his arms and took him into the bathroom and locked the door. Then nobody was shouting anymore, just Mama sitting on the floor with her shoulder leaned against the bathroom door, singing sweet words. Talking all kinds of sweetness to make my father come back out of that room and bring her baby with him. She was singing really beautiful through the door, so beautiful that I went to sleep and the next day and every other day we didn't talk about a treehouse anymore.

By the time it was three o'clock I had decided my talent was magic and I was itching for the bell to ring so I could go and see Ms. Clarkson. She's our school librarian but only on Tuesdays and Fridays, because the school doesn't have enough money to have a library open all week long. I was hoping she would have a book for me, maybe a secret book, even better. I was looking to produce the kind of show where things are disappearing and reappearing and girls are getting sawed in half. Yeah. And maybe some birds, trained birds that would fly out of my hands, which you previously thought were empty. I decided I needed a stage name that would tell you all that, and also it had to sound a little like my name, because credit where credit is due. Plus maybe a little continental. People always like a foreign name. *The Astonishing Arborio*, or *Abercrombus X*.

Ms. Clarkson had a book all right, but it was good and dog-eared, like some other guys had this idea before me. It was called *Best Magic Tricks for Kids to Learn* and mostly what it had were card tricks, which everyone knows are lame. There was one good vanishing trick in it, though, and all you needed was a toothpick and a ring. I thought if I figured out the trick of vanishing something small, like a toothpick, then maybe I could expand my knowledge and learn to vanish bigger things, like the dog or Peteyboy or Nana Louise. I laid the book across my handlebars and started reading up on the way home, going slow so I wouldn't get sick from reading and travelling like sometimes happens if you're taking a bus ride somewhere.

In a situation like that, the bike gets to have a mind of its own. My eyes were down in the magic book and not on the road and where the bike decided to go was right by that girl Madeleine's house. She and Geraldine were out in the yard playing at gymnastics on the swing set. The set had one regular swing, and then a high bar and a set of rings you could do flips on. Madeleine was hanging upside down from the high bar by her knees and letting her fingers scrape the ground and some of her hair was, too. The bottom of her shirt was doing a funny little flip thing. I noticed that my legs weren't working the pedals quite so fast. I rode a touch slower.

Madeleine yelled out to me, Well Abe, are you coming to my house for supper? and I yelled back Whatcha having? and she yelled Tripes à la mode de Caen! Tripes à la mode de Caen! and swung herself back and forth, upside down like that.

Geraldine screeched, Don't talk to him! and Madeleine swung her arms up and grabbed the bar and did a kind of somersault until she was on her feet. The bottom of her shirt flipped back so that it was flat against her stomach again. She came over near to where I had stopped my bike and stood there with both hands on the low fence and leaned over it toward me. She had some bits of old leaves sticking out of the ends of her hair. She sure looked sweet. She said, I bet I know something you don't know, Abe.

Yeah? I said. I folded up the book. I was about ready to get off my bike, too.

I heard a big truck came to your house this morning, Madeleine said, and took away all your Mama's things. She was combing her hair with her fingers to get the leaves out. She said: Your mother doesn't live with your Daddy anymore. She doesn't because she loves someone else now.

I looked her straight in the eye. I said, That sounds about right.

Madeleine said, I heard she came and sat in the truck while they packed up all her paintings and stuff and your father didn't even get out of bed to see her. He didn't even say her a goodbye.

I said, Geraldine, I hope you like fancy food. It sounds to me like you're going to get some good dinner over here with Madeleine.

Madeleine said, I'm sorry for you, Abe.

Well, I said. I've got some practicing to do if I'm gonna win that Pithog. I think I'll be going home. I stuck the book into my backpack and pushed off on my bike, standing up, you know how you do when you're really trying to get going somewhere.

We used to live in a different house that was close to where Grandpère lived, and in that house there wasn't any shabby shack for Mama to paint in and we lived with a different father then, too, our first father. When we lived in that house Peteyboy was just a baby so he usually doesn't remember too much about it, like when I say remember that old rope swing we used to have? Peteyboy nods and says yes, but there wasn't any rope swing because I just made that up. One thing that was different about that house is that when Mama went away she never left us there, she took us down the road to Grandpère's house until she came back. That's how I know about the tapes, because I used to help him set up his recorder every night and I saw the shoeboxes with their labels, *okay* and *mon cher*. She took us down the road because that other father couldn't look after us. If you were crying and standing up in your crib he might hit your face and make your nose bleed, which isn't really all right to do with a baby. When Mama was there he didn't do that stuff too much because she would make sure she was standing in the space between him and the crib.

These are the things I remember about that other father: he was tall, much taller than Mama, and his hair was black, like he'd combed it with ink or shoe black or something. He wore long-sleeved shirts with collars, but the sleeves were always rolled up short over his elbows and he wore wire-frame glasses and had a long, thin nose. He could play the violin and the piano and any kind of horn you gave him, so he was a lot of fun when there was a party at our house or any other house. He was someone Mama met when she was travelling and after she took us to live with our present father, he sold their house and went back to wherever he was from and didn't give her any of the money but she said she didn't want any of it anyway. Sometimes when I'm trying to think of things that happened around the time we left I get mixed up and forget which father did what, like all that treehouse stuff seems to me to belong to the first father but then since Peteyboy remembers it too, I know I must have it wrong. The father we have now is a bit more like a real dad that you see on television. He doesn't yell or scream too much, except he will lock you in your room, and when Madeleine says he didn't get out of bed to say goodbye I can believe it. Sometimes when I'm biking home I want to go down our old street and see Grandpère's house, but I don't do it because there's just a tiny part of me that wonders if my other father is still there in the old house and if he sees me he will remember that he loves me too much and will make me stay there and live with him instead.

I got home and dropped my bike around the side of the house. I walked into the backyard and let myself into the dusty shabby shack the way only I know how. Mama keeps a secret key under a rock three steps to the left and one down from the doorway. Where the daffodils come if it's April. She showed it to me once and said, Don't tell your father, don't tell anybody this is here, otherwise I'll never get any peace. They'll be forever walking in, asking me to taste this dish and see is it salty enough, or will I string some beads for them, or did I see whether the newspaper came yet. But she said I could come in anytime I liked, especially if she wasn't there. I put the key into the lock and let it sit in there a moment without turning or jiggling it and I just concentrated on my thoughts, and my thoughts were: Oh please.

Oh be there.

Go ahead and be there, all you paint pots and rags and old shirts Mama likes to wear when she's working. Just be there this one time and I will never again steal this key and sneak into this shack and I will never again ask her for nothing.

Never. Please.

Then I told myself Amen, because it seemed to me the

right way to end these thoughts.

But when I pushed open the door, true enough, there was nothing left. The shack seemed way smaller than it used to before, when it was full of stuff. Before, you could hardly move as you came in through the door. You thought you might knock something over and catch hell, but now that it was roomy and airy I could see just how tiny the place was. I could see why we called it the shabby shack.

There was just nothing.

A big ledge under the windows all spotted up with spilled paint. That's it.

I pulled the magic book out of my bag and set it up on the ledge. I reached into my fifth pocket and pulled out Mama's ring and from another pocket I got a clump of toothpicks that I found in the kitchen at school. I slipped the ring onto my finger, third finger, left hand. It fit pretty good. Her hands must be about the same size as mine, even though she's grown and I'm not. I wiggled it up and down on my finger but it wasn't loose enough to come right off, and that's all that matters where this trick is concerned.

This is how the trick works: You hold up the toothpick so everyone can see that you've got one. Then you wave your hand up and down real slow to distract your audience, but while you're waving you kinda push the toothpick down the back of your finger, between your skin and the ring. Then the ring holds it there nice and tight, and you can spread your fingers and show the spectators how it's not in your hand anymore. Pretty neat, huh?

At first I had to go real slow and easy and not do too much waving, but after about an hour I noticed that my fingers were moving a whole lot faster and by the time the sun was going down I didn't really have to think about what

I was doing anymore. My fingers could do the walking.

I thought about some other things instead.

I made up some stories.

I made up one story I liked. It went like this: One day, maybe a month from now, maybe a little more, Mama sends for me. She sends a taxicab to get me and a note that says, Abe you better come and see me right now and please don't forget to bring your old guitar because a girl can use some music when she's feeling low. So I pack up my suitcase and my guitar and load them into the taxicab and the driver takes it all over to Mama's new house. I don't ride in the cab because I'm following behind him on my Pithog. When I get to the new house, which is white and shiny and just what you think it should be, Mama is sitting there on the couch with a lace hankie and she does look burnt. She says, Abe, I sent him away. I had no choice. That man wouldn't cook for me! And I remember how she used to like it when I made her a cup of tea and crispy toast with a slice of ham on it, and I say, Mama, let's celebrate. Mama, I'm going to make you some kind of fancy dinner. She says, Abe, what are we having? and I say, Why, Tripes à la mode de Caen, of course! Mama says, Tripes à la mode de Caen! My very favourite thing! Thank goodness you're here! Do you know that man wouldn't even look at Tripes! He wouldn't even let me have Tripes in the house! And I say, Well that's all over now, Mama, and I get cooking and we have a great old time just eating and talking and laughing about things, and then after dinner I show her my repertoire of magic tricks. Starting with the vanishing toothpick, which is the first trick I ever learned.

I thought I'd show Peteyboy my trick, since I had got so good at it. I didn't have far to look for him. He was up in his tree again, even though it was pretty late. I climbed up onto his branch with a big flourish and shouted Behold! the Astonishing Abercrombie! and I began to perform for him. I was humming a little tune, because there's always music when they show magic on TV. I got to the end part and spread my fingers out to show the toothpick had absolutely vanished into thin air.

Peteyboy said, Toothpick's pretty hard to see if you're sitting way back in the gym. Toothpick's pretty skinny, he said. You almost don't have to work to vanish a toothpick. It's almost not there already.

I told him a toothpick's just nothing, a toothpick's just the beginning. I told him I was going to learn how to vanish him soon. Or the shabby shack. Or the future.

I told him how I saw Madeleine Welsher playing at gymnastics. I told him about the flippy thing her shirt could do.

Peteyboy just kept on looking down the road.

Nobody knows the future, he said.

Then he climbed down out of the tree and went across the yard and into the house.

I guess he went to bed.

After we moved to this new house, I saw our other father one last time. I was playing around the side of the yard. It was almost dark. Peteyboy must have been in bed already, but I was outside looking at bugs and doing other things that little kids do. A truck pulled up into the driveway and Mama came out of the house and got into the truck and sat in the passenger side talking to that other father, who was driving. I started to go to the truck too, because I thought maybe she was going home and then I could go with her. When I got closer I could see that they weren't really talking at all. Mama had her mouth pressed against his temple and her workshirt was bunched funny with his arm up underneath it and I could see his hand on her body, her breasts loose like she was going to bed. And then she pushed his hand down and smoothed his hair out of his face and kissed both his cheeks and got out of the truck, and he backed it away down the drive and she called to me and took me inside for a bath.

I was thinking about that when I watched Peteyboy going inside to bed. He's always going to bed before me, and missing things.

He'd left his tape recorder and headphones balancing up in the tree. I put the headphones on. They made it sound like you were sitting under a blanket. There was an old tape in the machine and I hit *record*. The little wheels started turning.

I stayed up on that branch for a long time still, just looking down the road. There wasn't much moon, so there wasn't much to see. You could hear the new frogs all singing from the ditch behind the house. In the spring the rainwash fills up the ditch until it's almost like a pond, and that's where all the frogs get born. And sing and sing.

I thought about what I should call the tape, should I call it *okay* or *mon cher*. My legs were hanging down off the branch. It felt like my feet could touch the ground from up there. If I was that tall, my hands could reach higher than the top branches. I'd be able to see everything and everyone, and nothing would happen without my knowing about it. I could understand what Peteyboy liked about being up in that tree. If you were that tall, everyone would know that you were magic. I thought that was about how tall the Astonishing Abercrombie should really be.

HOW TO GET ALONG
WITH WOMEN

At night she takes him walking.

I'm wondering, she says. Is there anything you want to tell me?

They are close to the hedge line on the narrow sidewalk. His arm scrapes up against everyone's garden.

I mean, she says. I guess I mean, is there anything you want me to do? Playing at his hand, but not holding it. Smacking it lightly.

What do you think about? she says.

Like right now? he says. This is not what she means.

Smack, smack.

Then: Do you want to know what I think about?

Sure, he says.

No, really. Do you.

Of course I do, he says.

They took the two-bedroom because it was only another hundred a month. The first day she practiced hiding in all the closets and called his name to see if he could hear her. His father with the truck full of boxes. Her parents with a bedframe packed in styrofoam. You've set up shop! Good to see, good to see. Pawing at his hand for a shake. Then his own father climbing back in the empty truck and the new semester about to start.

Yellow kerchief over her hair, greasy smear of dirt under one eye.

Not dirt. Cake mix. A new-house cake while he scrubs the blue toilet. If he stands just outside the doorway, scrub brush dripping from one hand, he can watch her lever her body under the sink. Hip slipping up and out of the waistband of her jeans.

He says, Is it weird your parents bought us a bed?

A bowl-shaped cake because they don't have a pan.

Okay, she says.

Her hand slapping at his arm, and the hedge on the other side, and him in between.

Okay, sometimes. I'm in this stark white room, a big room, with bright lights and a table, like an operating room. There's maybe five or six men in there with me, but only one is in charge. The rest are like interns.

Is it a hospital? he says. His parents are doctors.

No. It just feels like a hospital. Anyway, the guy who's in charge gets the other younger men to do things to me.

What things, he says. What do you mean, things.

Everything, she says. All at once. Like, one of them's got his cock in my mouth and one's inside me and one's in my ass. Like that. And the whole thing's being filmed, and there's this big screen against the wall, and I have to watch myself get fucked in all these impossible ways, over and over again.

Do you know the men?

No. No, I'm like a volunteer. Like the actors who pretend

to be sick so interns can learn how to be doctors.

Doctors again, he thinks.

So? she says.

So, what.

So, see? She grabs his hand. Now you know.

Okay.

So. What do you think about.

He considers lying. Something-something feather dusters. Anal rape.

Mostly, he says. Mostly I just think about you.

She was born here, but her parents are refugees. She never says immigrants. She grew up in the east end in a house with a concrete pad instead of a yard. She's never been to summer camp. She's never camped at all. She went to finishing school on Saturday mornings for two years running, when she was seven and eight years old.

What do you do at finishing school? he said when she told him this. His own parents sent him to Junior Rangers up in Grégoire's Mill when he was sixteen.

Oh, you know, you learn to clean your nails, you give yourself a nice manicure, you walk with a book on your head—

He thought she was joking. That exists?

Oh, yes.

She speaks four languages: one to her parents, one to her grandmother, English to him, and another besides, just for the sake of it. Her father says, With languages, you can never go wrong. After the war her father went to France and became an army interrogator, living in the Vienna French Quarter and questioning suspected Nazi sympathizers in four languages.

She plays the piano and the cello. She wanted to play the flute but she wasn't allowed.

My father said playing the flute deforms your lips, like this. She sticks her lips out in a way that makes her look inexpressibly sad. Then you're not so beautiful.

He plays the trumpet and his mother plays the piano. At Christmas his mother likes to play carols. She accompanies him, or the other way around.

He is two years behind her at school. He moved to London to be with her rather than because he cares about university. He is majoring in Horticulture. His parents wonder if he wouldn't like to switch to Bio-Med.

She worries that, living with her, he will miss out on the first year experience.

How will you make your own friends? she says. Don't you want to live in residence, just for a year?

She works for the student paper. On Tuesdays, she works all night.

Don't move here just for me, she says. Move here because you want to.

What if what I want is to be with you?

He is minoring in German.

She doesn't want him sitting home waiting for her. She doesn't want to have to think of that on Tuesday nights.

He taught her how to get in a canoe. He taught her how to play croquet. She likes cross-country skiing better than downhill because it's an endurance test and because he told her how his mother had skiing accidents two years in a row when he was a child. The first time she met his parents, the mother hiked her skirt up to the thighs to show the surgeon's scars: one over each knee.

It ruined my legs, the mother said.

When she was waiting for surgery his father marked the ripped knee with a Sharpie. He drew a black arrow pointing down and wrote the words THIS KNEE.

It was kind of a joke, he said. But I work in hospitals.

She has a little red kilt she bought at the Mission du Grand Berger in Montreal. She goes into the bedroom and fools around with clothes for a while: the kilt, long white socks, a white blouse tied up tight under her small breasts. The schoolgirl routine seems not enough. There's an eye mask she uses for sleeping during the day. She looks at herself in the mirror, this way and that. When she comes out he's asleep on the couch and she wakes him up.

What's going on, he says.

Later he finds her reading and says, I just figured it out. I was sleeping and—

It's okay, she says, waving her bookmark at him. It's okay, it's okay.

He makes friends without being in residence. He makes friends with other first year students who are already in their twenties, studying computers and business management, practical things they think will get them jobs. On Tuesday nights he sits in the campus bar with Claire and Ben and plays the trivia game. The most common form of hyperthyroidism is better known as _____ Disease. Alzheimer's Coats' Graves' Lou Gehrig's. The time ticking down, answers slipping off the screen. Sometimes he would rather be at home, reading, but he knows this would bother her.

At the newspaper, her section is usually done first. Some

people are still writing on Tuesday nights, but she can't cope with a missed deadline. If the art is ready, she's done by midnight, but stays for the three a.m. banter, the pizza, the strange sandwiches the photo editor brings her from Mr. Sub stacked with strips of green pepper and black olives. She's never ordered food all-dressed. My parents are refugees, she says. She has never eaten an onion ring.

When the photo editor offers to get her a club soda, she is delighted.

She doesn't like pop. She's had Coke and Pepsi and Orange. She's never had Doctor Pepper. She's never had Mountain Dew.

In the winter he drives her up to his father's cabin in the truck with their skis strapped to the top. The cabin is small and heated by a woodstove and she sits on the edge of the bed holding a mitten over her nose to keep it from freezing. There is no toilet. His mother doesn't come to the cabin because she doesn't like places where there is nothing to do. So the cabin is not used to women.

There is an outhouse and a jar to pee in at night. She crouches with her feet on the icy floor while he lies in bed just above her. The jar has a slim mouth and she pees on her fingers, all over the floor, but it's so cold you can't smell it.

The next night she takes the jar into the other room.

Her father likes him. When her father comes to London to pick them up for Christmas break, he calls him boytchik instead of his name. He calls him the Bearded Wonder. They eat lunch together at an Indian restaurant, then her father throws their stuff—his hiker's pack, her duffle bag—into the trunk of the Corolla. A two-and-a-half hour drive.

She sits up front with her father and plays with the vents and the radio.

He sits in the back. For three weeks he will live at his old house and she at hers. On the way home the Bearded Wonder rolls down his window, sticks his head out and howls like a dog.

She's never seen a bear. She's never seen a moose. When her cousin came to visit from Kyiv he spent an hour chasing squirrels on the lawn at Queen's Park because there are no squirrels in Eastern Europe.

She's never seen a beaver. How about in the museum? she asks him. Stuffed. Does that count?

No.

Then, no.

She's never had a hot dog.

But you were born here! he says.

When I was in grade one, she says, I used to walk home from school for lunch. I could smell the hot dogs boiling in other houses and I'd think, I wonder what my house is cooking? Probably borscht.

She has a cousin in Salzburg. She has a cousin in Zurich. She has a cousin in Dresden. She has a cousin in Grenoble. She has a cousin in Copenhagen. She has a cousin in Dubrovnik. She has a cousin in Gdansk.

She's sitting on the couch at his parents' house. He tells her that when his mother curls up to read, her whole body fits on one cushion.

Like this?

No, he says. Your feet are still on the other cushion.

Like this?

I think you're too tall, baby.

Like this?

When his mother leans forward to serve the soup at dinner, she tries to gauge the size of her breasts. Whose breasts are bigger?

Do you even want to finish this degree? she says. Don't do it just because your parents want you to. Don't feel you have to do anything. Your problem is all your mother, she says. Push push push.

On Saturday night she goes to the photo editor's house to watch the fights on pay-per-view. Do you want to come, she says on her way out the door.

Do I have to say yes, he says from the couch.

The fight ring surprises her. It's an octagon. The cage has no ceiling. She expected something different.

Is it gory? she asks in advance. Will I be upset?

Sometimes someone gets a broken arm, the photo editor says, and her eyes brighten. Not every time, he says.

The other editors are there: the news editor, the sports editor, the entertainment editor. The programming director from the campus radio station is there. She is the only girl. They eat Cheetos and drink canned beer.

Between fights she tells them a story. A man dies, she says, and in the afterlife he finds himself sitting at a table with a beer in his hand and a girl on his lap. There's another man sitting on the other side of the table, same deal. The dead guy says, This must be heaven! His friend says, Nope. Hell. The dead guy says, How can you say that? His friend says, Easy. There's a hole in the bottom of the beer, and no hole in the bottom of the girl.

When she gets home he is in bed watching an old movie with Fred Astaire and Ginger Rogers tap dancing and singing about potatoes. Astaire doing his best Russian accent. The one where they are on a boat.

Who's that, she says. On screen, Ginger Rogers on rollerskates.

Knockout? he says.

The newsroom is an old boys' club, she tells him, crawling in.

On Saturday night he goes out for coffee with Claire. Claire is short and curvy with curly hair, she grew up in Orillia and for years was a lifeguard at a provincial park and wore one of those red shirts with a big white cross on it. She has a boyfriend who drives in every two weeks for a couple days. She wants him to explain the boyfriend. They've got a box of those round, powdery donuts between them, what the coffee shops used to call leftover donut holes.

Why does the boyfriend always want her to masturbate in front of him, Claire wants to know. Why does he want to ejaculate in her face. She has a little powdered sugar caught in her hair.

It's that you are probably so sweet to him, he says. He can't imagine anything sweeter than you, so he can't imagine anything dirtier than coming in your sweet, sweet face.

Claire nods slowly, chewing. She chews one donut hole for a long time.

I'm really sorry, he says.

Later he walks Claire back to her room. They practice their German for the oral exam.

Wie geht's dir?
Geht's mir sehr gut.
Willst du noch ein Kaffee?
Danke schön.
Bitte schön.
He calls home but she isn't there.

The house where his parents live has three stories, a bathtub on every floor. Where she grew up there was one bathroom, a shower stall, no grass. All her parents' money went back home. Her father sent money orders in US dollars to the orthodox Popa and trusted him to use it for the village. Every summer they went back to Europe and stayed for six weeks.

We'd arrive in Paris, she says. As soon as the plane touched down, we'd start driving. We flew all night and then my father drove all day. Once I fell asleep in the car and when I woke up my father was slapping himself to stay awake. He wouldn't let my mother drive the car because it was a standard and he was afraid she'd stall it at the border crossing and draw attention to us.

They drove from Paris to Switzerland, and then to Austria, Hungary, and into the Ukraine, staying with relatives in every country.

Everyone went west, she says. As far as they could. But no one came as far as us.

You couldn't get coffee behind the Iron Curtain. You couldn't get chocolate. Her aunt in Hungary didn't go to church because her uncle had joined the party.

In Austria we stopped at the Metro store and loaded the car with coffee and chocolate, to bring as presents, she says. There was one whole aisle of just chocolate. In Ukraine my mother always thought someone was following us. The public pool was a natural bath and the water was dark brown from iodine.

She shows him a picture of herself at sixteen.

Wearing a wedding dress.

It's not a wedding dress, she says. It's my debut. I was a debutante.

The picture was taken in the ballroom of an old hotel. There are fourteen other girls, also wearing wedding dresses, and a number of men in their early twenties wearing tuxedoes.

They hire these guys, she says, from the university or somewhere, to be escorts for the debutantes.

This was your date? he says, pointing to a short man wearing horn-rimmed glasses.

Yeah, she says. But I really liked this guy. Pointing to a blond vampire.

Her friend's escort.

He was from Biarritz, she says. My friend told me, If you steal my date, I'll never speak to you again.

That's too bad, he says. I'm sure he was quite a gentleman. He's seen a lot of her pictures. She doesn't seem to have had any real boyfriends. He lost his virginity when he was sixteen to a girl he'd been dating for a year. He's told her that story, and the one about the Texan girl the winter he was a ski instructor, her half-shaved head and swimmer's shoulders, how she could hold him down.

He took me behind the stage and fingered me under my dress, she says.

But your friend.

I knew she'd speak to me again.

The next Saturday fight night, she comes home drunk. He is

sitting in the kitchen with a plate of crackers and Hungarian salami and reading a science fiction novel.

Hey baby, she says. Can I try your salami? She is wearing one shoe and peels her sweater up over her head.

I'm pretty tired, he says, and she stamps her shoe on the linoleum, hard.

I work with nine guys every day of my life, she says.

He says he knows.

I don't know what's wrong with me, he says.

In the spring he gets a night job and they move into his parents' basement in Toronto. She likes it because it's a good neighbourhood and she can pretend she's their daughter and not a refugee. She lies in the backyard hammock drinking coffee and looking at the big red canoe turned bottom up against the fence.

His cousin Jessica gets her a job but she quits after two days.

They said I was overqualified, she tells him. They said I'd be really bored.

She doesn't know how to get along with women, Jessica says.

His father likes her. His brother likes her. At dinner his brother says she is like the sister he never had and his cousin Jessica says, Watch it. The brother has an opera-singing girlfriend and a diabetic cat. When it's spring break he fractures his collarbone and can't comb his own hair. He waits to take a shower until everyone else has left the house, then finds her in the living room, reading. Would she comb through his wet hair. He holds a towel around his waist, bare feet sinking into the carpet. His hair comes past his shoulders.

I want to wake up and find you already inside me, she says. Like you don't even care that I'm sleeping. Do you think you could do that?

I love you, he says. And that sounds like rape.

There's a radio conference in Ottawa. The program director at her campus station invites her, puts her on a panel as an expert on student activism. It's you and three white guys with beards, the program director tells her. She waits around afterward to talk to the moderator, a media studies professor named Julien Paré. There are three students with him and she is aware of her flat, ugly shoes. Why did she bring these shoes to Ottawa? One of the students asks if he has seen the new movie about cross-dressers hitchhiking their way through middle America and she interrupts without thinking. We're so busy congratulating ourselves, she says. Everything new is boring.

I'd like to buy you a drink, Paré says.

She orders a Campari-soda and talks to him about student media, foreign film, her ideas about subtitling. What she really wants is to write and produce radio documentaries, but she doesn't know how to get in at the CBC. She describes her apartment in London. Paré once taught a session at Western; he lived in the same building.

You have one of those L-shaped one-bedrooms, he says.

A two-bedroom, she says. We wanted more space.

So you already have a room for the baby, he says. How about a station wagon? Do you have that, too? He looks at her intently. All her plans are childish.

Come on, he says. I'm only teasing. Young women have to be serious. I rely on you. If the young women cease their seriousness, we are lost.

We're living in Rosedale for the summer, she says. We're very different. He grew up with one of those names everyone knows how to pronounce.

He takes her to a strip bar. The waitresses are all topless.

I hope you aren't uncomfortable, he says.

I wish my breasts were closer together, she says, chewing on her straw.

I'd like you to write me some letters, Paré says. Will you do that?

They are in his parents' kitchen frying onions for pierogy. Listen, she says. There's something I want to ask you.

Cher M. Paré,

A few evenings ago I had a dream about you. We were in the largest music library in the world. You were talking to me about libretti. I was carrying a boning knife.

She doesn't cry when she chops onions because her contact lenses protect her eyes. He is wearing an apron so that the flour doesn't get everywhere.

I want to know how you'd feel, she says. I have this opportunity. To sleep with a much older man, just for the experience, would that be all right with you? If it was just sex. Just for the experience.

He's got the bowl of dough under one arm and a wooden spoon tight in his fingers. It takes more strength than you'd imagine to mix dough by hand. All the tendons in his forearm stretched and tingling. He stops stirring and thinks for a moment.

No, he says. No, I don't think that would be all right.

I think he knows but he doesn't know, she says. But if he knows, why doesn't he ask any questions.

Lots of men are like that, Paré says, rolling over to look at the time. He has a meeting in an hour.

An old friend of mine, he says. Moved up to head of English programming for eastern Canada. I used to play hockey with him in the alley behind our houses. His father was Minister of Transportation in the seventies, we could go to the yacht club and eat all the cheeseburgers we wanted.

She has a file on her laptop of scripts, pitches that she has never sent to Paré.

Cheeseburgers and milkshakes, he says. Old friends are wonderful. I'll have to tell him I know a really sharp young writer he should be looking at.

She can't breathe.

One of my students, he says. Brought me a script on Friday. I've been coaching him from day one.

He folds himself over and sinks his teeth into her ass.

There is a house up the street from where his parents live now that he lived in as a child. They inherited it from his grandparents, so it's the same house the father grew up in. His parents moved down the street when he was fifteen.

We should buy that house, she says. Then when we have a boy, he could grow up there, too.

The idea of producing a boy, or of not being a boy himself, alarms him.

We could never afford it, he says, and she looks disappointed. Later he draws a little cartoon for her, two stick figures and a bassinet with a ? over top of it. He leaves it on her pillow when he goes to work.

She eats dinner slowly in the hotel bar, then takes the long streetcar ride back to his parents' house at night. His shift starts at eleven. He is already gone when she gets back. His mother and father are sitting on the porch. His father offers her a beer. His mother offers her canned peaches, ice cream.

He works nights on the cleaning crew at the hydro plant. Once when he was shoving garbage into a dumpster something sharp cut his hand and he had to have shots for hepatitis C. He wears a blue uniform with someone else's name on it, because he's just covering vacations. In September he is supposed to finish his degree but now that they're here, he doesn't like the thought of going back to London. It's a small town compared to what he's used to, and he likes it here. His old friends from high school and the same bars they always went to.

Before work he has a beer with Colin and Mercer and tells them about Claire, her boyfriend.

Colin's girlfriend won't let him come in her face, either. Mercer once pretended to slip in the shower so that his girlfriend would take it up the ass.

She kept saying she didn't want to try it, Mercer says. So we were doing it in the shower and I slipped.

I just wanted to try it once, Mercer says.

The constant negotiation for sex makes his friends tired. It makes him tired, too, but in a different way: he'd rather avoid her, sleep during the day than have to talk about it. The job at Hydro makes him happy. He knows when to show up, when to leave, what to do when he gets there.

When she goes down to the basement she finds a note, the little drawing on the bed. She flips her pillow so that the note falls off. She can pretend she hasn't seen it.

He gets home after seven in the morning and she doesn't wake up. He's been thinking about Mercer all night, and Colin, and what to say when she stamps her feet on the ground. She looks like a different girl, sleeping. Not pretty. She doesn't look sweet. Once she fell asleep watching Bugs Bunny with her head in his lap and drooled all over his pant leg.

He takes off the uniform with the other guy's name on it and folds it, then rolls it into a ball and throws it at the hamper. Nothing wakes her up until he moves into her. With her eyes open she looks much younger than she is. She looks like a kid in the schoolyard getting beaten up. She opens her mouth like she might say something, so he puts his hand over her face and keeps on.

YOU KNOW HOW I FEEL

Ruby refuses to sleep until after Sudbury. I want to be buried in suds, she says. I want a bubble bath in Sud-Buried.

It's six hours in the car and they don't even stop. Gas, once. The car's a rental, small and zippy and silver. Great pick-up: what the rent-a-car man said, handing over the keys. You get out on the highway and give 'er. There's a bounce to the gearshift, or Sarah bounces it. Out on the highway she gives 'er, and they stay in fifth for three hours straight. They left at five in the morning so Ruby would sleep.

Sarah doesn't have a car seat for her. Why should she? They never take a car in the city. And Ruby's got to be forty pounds by now or close to it, and anyway, didn't we all ride across the country without car seats in the 70s?

Glenna will be horrified.

Glenna will be charmed by this and tell and retell the story at dinner that night. Silas, pick that child up and tell me she's forty pounds. Sarah, we will give you a car seat, we'll *give* it to you. We must have an old one around here somewhere.

How many at dinner. Sarah and Ruby. Glenna, Silas, their three boys, her two parents. Plus plus plus. Some assortment of others, friends or almost-cousins or whoever else Glenna can pull in for a week away. Drunk Silas, his arm snaked around Sarah's waist, hand under her clothes. The same the last two summers: Sarah changing into pyjamas in the safety of her locked car, Silas wandering the lawn at two in the morning. Ruby asleep, waiting for Sarah in the tent.

We're very lucky, Sarah says out loud. We get a whole bunkhouse to ourselves. Like a cabin. Like a fort, she says.

How about we sleep in a tent? Ruby says.

No, Sarah says. A bunkhouse. A little house for just us. She flicks her eyes up to the rearview. But we can put a special net over your bed to keep the mosquitoes away.

Like a tent? Ruby says.

Like a canopy, Sarah says. Like a princess.

She sprays some wiper fluid and sets the arms going on the windshield. Ruby closes her eyes and tips down toward the bench in the backseat.

In Sud-Buried I will have a creamy bath of round, pink bubbles, she says. And a princess bed with a beautiful lace tent.

Silas is out in the gravel drive when they pull in, smoking a joint where Glenna can't see him. Bent over a bike tire to make it look like he's doing something. Watching, Sarah thinks, for this car. For Sarah and Ruby.

Beckett!

He pinches the roach tight between his fingers, slides it into the breast pocket of his shirt. A strong, fast hug, his arms wrapped firm around her back and then gone. Sarah springs the hatch and starts hauling gear out onto the ground: duffle bags, the cooler, a sleeping bag in case they need it. Silas pops the passenger door.

Hey Ruby-Ruby! Pushes a finally-sleepy Ruby along toward the cottage and comes back for Sarah.

Took you long enough, Beckett.

Sarah points to the sleeping bag. Silas shakes his head and she throws it back in the car and slams the door.

I forgot you're a betting man, she says. I hate to disappoint.

I had forty dollars on you at 10:30.

Five-year-old in the back, remember.

Five, shmive, Silas says. You've cost me. How about a drink.

Is it noon?

Different rules up here, my friend.

How many, Sarah says, meaning rules or guests, whatever Silas comes up with first.

Let's see. Silas half-shuts one eye in the manner of the thinking man. There's us and you. That's seven, if you include children. Do we?

Yes.

All right then. Seven. Glenna's parents. Nine. Mike and Ilsa. You met them once in the city.

He never talks, Sarah says. Why doesn't he ever talk?

He's a mute, of course. All the best men are. Silas pauses. They have a baby now, it's awful, you can't stand it, don't talk to Ilsa if you can help it. So what's that?

Twelve, Sarah says.

With children.

Yes, with.

Seven without, Silas says.

But we get the bunkhouse still, Sarah says. Me and Ruby, that hasn't changed. She leans down and takes a bag in each hand.

Is that a good thing?

It's good. It's good for Ruby, Sarah says. Of course it means I can't even jerk off by myself.

If only you'd learn to keep your mouth shut, Silas says.

The screen door slaps shut and Glenna is outside, her blonde hair pulled back smooth and clean, wearing a blue one-piece, Sarah can see, under her dress.

Sarah, Glenna says.

She holds Sarah by the elbows.

At dinner Silas announces: Beckett's a poet!

The others at table shift in their seats. What now?

Glenna: We all know her, Silas.

Not Mike and Ilsa. Mike, did you know Beckett writes poems? Books and everything.

Ilsa, Sarah says to distract from the unsettling business of her own poem-writing. The bottle stands by you.

Ilsa is short and pretty, with red hair tied up in a knot of bobby pins. She's round in a way that Sarah admires. Imagine being round like that, Sarah thinks. Imagine that belly. She perceives fat women not as happy, exactly, but perhaps blithe. Free of doubt. The blanket of flesh between their hips also insulating against too much thinking.

Sarah pours and Silas pouts at his end of the table. Oh come on, Beckett.

I haven't got any stories.

Men.

There haven't been any, Sarah says. I'm shamefully celibate. I went out with one, for dinner. He was married. I was almost sure he was married when he asked me. I went so I could prove it to myself.

Do you know when I met Beckett? Silas turns to Mike, who twitches with alarm at the attention. Have I told this story? New Year's Eve. He looks wildly around, suddenly discovering Sarah again. You had that crazy house with all the stairs. Ruby was only toddling.

Sarah nods at her own glass. She was in diapers.

Oh, I don't know, Silas says. Glenna, where were you. Why was I there alone.

I went home, Glenna says.

Right, Silas says. His shirt cuffs are unbuttoned and the flapping sleeves give him the look of a fallen duke—as though the estate could be seized at any time. I meant to go, too, he says, but it was blackout time and, and everything went dark kind of. I come to, and I'm on this white, white couch in a white living room. I thought, Is this the mental ward or what, but when I looked around and saw all the things, you know, the accessories, they were so nice.

Glenna lays a hand flat on the table: Silas. That's enough.

So I wake up and I hear some girl and guy just beating the shit out of each other you know? That was Beckett and Marcus. Right, Beckett? But she didn't seem like one of those ladies tied to the tracks, I didn't have to rescue her. So I ostriched it. Like this, I went back to sleep. Silas folds his hands into a pillow and settles down for a moment next to his dinner plate, then bobs back up. She was giving good as she got, he says. And I wake up a few hours later with some little blondie bouncing around on me. Happy New Year! Happy New Year! That was Ruby. And I sat up, Hello, and there were all these people around I didn't know and here's Beckett: lalala! mojitos! shrimp ring! Silas pushes his hair back with one hand and grips the table-edge with the other, holding himself down.

I ended up staying for two days, he says. Beckett wouldn't let me go! I stayed for two days eating fucking shrimp ring.

Two days, Glenna says, wine glass in hand. And Sarah was the one who got a divorce.

So you're co-parenting. Ilsa turns to Sarah. That's good. I mean, you have your independence. The grass is always greener, right?

It's like being a homeless person, Sarah says. You never know where your next meal is coming from.

Silas: What are you talking about down there, Beckett. Are you talking about fucking.

In my next marriage, Glenna says, I think I'll be the reckless one.

Mike gives Ilsa a hard look.

Sarah turns to Glenna. Where's Ruby? Is she in bed?

Glenna's mother took Ruby for a pedal boat in the afternoon. A kind of pity. People are always wanting Sarah to take time off. As though parenting were some new and difficult task when really it has always been just her and Ruby.

We're all done with kids! Silas says to the room and his sleeve catches the rim of a glass, sending a spray of shiraz across the tablecloth.

Salt! Glenna jumps up.

White wine! Silas yells and grabs for Mike's glass.

Sarah's own glass is empty again. To Ilsa she says, He was away, working on a play. Anyway he was away a lot.

I shot my guns in the air for a while, Sarah says.

The men start stacking dishes, apart from Silas who leans on one hand.

Are a lot of them married?

Shocking, Sarah says. Isn't it.

It's not, Ilsa says. Take a look at you. Men always think they're entitled, but really. I fetishize your breasts. I secretly love your breasts.

Mike, in the kitchen with dishes, takes on a look of resignation.

You don't seem to be afraid of any of it, Ilsa says.

Glenna's mother calls from outdoors: Someone's baby's crying! But it's a loon, they realize it as soon as Ilsa has run from the room.

In the morning there are cheese omelettes. Sarah shows Ruby how to wash her feet in the water bucket by the door. There's a bucket by every door, she says. No sandy toes in the house, okay?

She pulls a kayak down into the water. Silas on the dock, plate in hand, heels together. His back to her: a kind of lameness in the way he stands. He's softened in the way married men do, men who feel somewhat guaranteed. Sarah with her notebook in a zippered plastic bag in case of a spill. She wades out to the knees and climbs in, gripping the bag between her thighs, and paddles quickly. It's a small lake and she wants to be out in it, far enough to blur anything familiar, the children shrieking at their dock wars. She'd woken early and boiled water for coffee, watched Glenna's parents steal a kiss in the lean-to, the old man stuffing a pipe with tobacco. Honey, they called each other. Sarah watching, rubbing the tender insides of her wrists together in the kitchen window.

She comes around an outcrop of rock and pine, Crown land, thick with brush, and into the bay. Sets the paddle carefully across the open seat of the kayak and pulls the notebook out from between her legs. It's hot and still on the water. She tugs the brim of her straw hat down lower around her face. High up, there are white clouds moving fast: now sunny, now shade. Now sun again.

Marcus when they were first together, blond hair falling over his eyes, dancing wild around her room. The back of his t-shirt a wet V. What Mozart would look like, Sarah said, if he were born in 1971. Washing dishes in Sarah's sink wearing her pink rubber gloves. Sarah naked in the kitchen, poaching eggs, beating the linoleum with her red patent heels. At night they ran down the stairs and traced thick chalk outlines of themselves beneath the balcony, waited up until morning to see the look on the Italian Nonna who lived next door and watered her tubs of plastic roses until mould curled around the edges of the leaves. In bed Sarah held a pen and tried to work while Marcus twined her hair around his fingers and ran his hand along her ribcage and squeezed at her nipples underneath her shirt and nudged her thighs apart with his own knee and took away the book and slapped at the pen and slid his hands beneath her hips and stroked into her cleanly twice and three times and then stopped until she asked him and asked him again to please, please make her come.

The kayak smacks up against something and Sarah grabs at the paddle. It's shady and cool. She looks down and there are rocks. Shallows. The brim of the hat pulled so low that she didn't see how far she'd drifted, aground, cool not because of clouds, but because of shade, the cast of trees above her.

She wedges the book back between her knees and pushes off firmly with the paddle, kayak scraping the stony lake floor, then out of the bay and toward open water. Her shoulders stiff with sun. Sitting up taller, she pushes the paddle deep, twirling it on every stroke until she's moving swift and clean. This brings the wind up, or the feel of it. Where is Ruby. Sarah can't see her from this bend. Someone has her, certainly, has given her a sensible lunch. She slacks off and listens to her breath, hard and fast. The paddle crossways, resting lightly in the crease between thumbs and forefingers.

There's a cry and Sarah sees the loon. It's the male, twenty feet to the right of her. Then only ten. Close. Does he know she's a boat. He dips under the surface and Sarah counts, but he doesn't come up. Then she sees him, around the other side of the kayak. Maybe three or four minutes under water. He lets a cry loose over the lake and the echo rings back, the sound like another bird calling. Tucked in an inlet, the female is quiet, busy with her babies. Fish in mouth, he calls again, twitches in the direction of the echo.

You're not calling to her at all, Sarah says out loud.

She dips the paddle and moves closer.

That loon killed a beaver this time last year, Glenna says.

She's out on the dock as Sarah paddles in, page-turner in hand, creamy layer of sunscreen not quite soaked into the skin on her thighs. He came up from underneath. Their beaks are like scissors, you know. Beaver shot straight up into the air. People saw it across the bay.

I seemed to make him nervous, Sarah says. She hauls the kayak up where the dirt is dry-baked, flips it so the bottom-side glints in the sun. It's not a heavy boat, but it catches in the long grass. Sarah's shoulders and thin spine showing as she tugs it into place, her slim legs curving out from the bottom of her bathing suit.

He just doesn't want you close to his family, that's all, Glenna says.

Where's Ruby?

She's on ride-along. My dad took her to the dump. I think she's hoping to catch a bear. Glenna sets the book down and raises a hand to shade her eyes. He's been feeding her stories about how we live in the Bear Capital of the World.

Did she eat? Sarah picks up the tube of sunscreen and squirts a sausage of white into her hand, rubs this into her belly and under the band of her bikini top, then around the back of her neck.

We made sandwiches. Jesus there's nothing on you, is there?

It's an optical illusion, Sarah says. I'm heavier than I look. She sets the cream back on the table and falls into a chair. Was I gone long? I'm working something up in my head, sometimes I lose track of time.

We've got Ruby. Glenna pulls her feet and ankles onto the chair and sits curled up. You mean working like writing-working.

Like that, yes.

I was worried you were upset, Glenna says. Because of Silas, you know. He should keep his stories to himself. Her ankles are crossed. Sarah can see the first hint of sunburn on her breastbone, the skin ruddy and loose-looking.

Oh, about Marcus, she says. Sarah takes off the hat and shakes her hair out. It's all right. It's what happened, right? I used to say if it were high school, I'd have broken up with Marcus a thousand times.

Glenna tilts her head a moment.

I look at you and Silas, Sarah says. Do you think I'll ever get my shit together.

Silas gets drunk, Glenna says. It's his fatal flaw. I look across the room and see him dancing sexy with some girl and I just go home.

Why don't you dance, Sarah says. If he wants to.

He only thinks it's what he wants.

Sarah looks down at her sprawling legs. Something about

Glenna makes her feel gangly, pubescent, too naked.

I wish I'd left Marcus years ago, she says.

From the other side of the house there's a motor, there are tires on gravel, voices.

You know what I think? Glenna stands up and wraps a towel around her waist. All of us, we all do the things we really want to. I believe that. So all that wishful talk, I wish you'd do this or that, I wish I'd married the kind of girl that will dance with me: it's just a way of excusing our own bad behaviour. It's the same with regret.

Sarah squints up. Glenna bends from the waist, gripping the towel with one hand, picks up her book.

Is that Ruby? Sarah says.

We've got Ruby, Glenna says. You just take care of yourself.

Sarah sits out on the dock a while longer, until the wind comes up and it's too cold to pretend to work anymore, even with her jeans pulled on over top of the bikini. She goes and lies down on the bed and her knees drop open. Unzips. Ruby is safely away.

She gets her hand going. It's not Marcus she thinks of, not anymore, not for a long time, but a kind of faceless stand-in. Blond still, but with a beard. Spare and muscled. A vein running down his forearm.

Whose cunt is it? Yours baby. Whose tits? Yours. Who owns you? You do, baby, you do. It's all for you, now let me come, please...

Through the particle board she can hear Mike and Ilsa, the baby crying.

When's it look like for dinner?

They're aiming at seven.

You can hear the clinking plates and that, so I guess it'll

be soon. Smells amazing. We could smell it out on the lake.

Take it, Sarah thinks, *take it*.

In the evening they take the children fishing: just Sarah and Silas. The rowboat loaded with rods, Ruby and the three boys, Sarah showing Ruby how to bisect a worm with her sharp fingernail and hook just a piece.

They're wiggling! Ruby squeals and pinches her own worm into two halves. All the pieces keep wiggling!

Glenna stays on the dock with her book, the others talking about a bonfire or cards. Glenna's mother with her long white hair twisted up and pinned at the neck, on the shore picking sticks, things to burn in the fire. Honey, she calls out, and the old man answers from the lean-to where he's got Glenna's bicycle up on a rack, fitting a new tube into the tire.

I'm sorry I told that story last night. Silas presses the rod handle, ready-cast, into Ruby's hand. Looks up at Sarah. About New Year's Eve. It wasn't fair.

Glenna?

Wouldn't fuck me because of it. He grins down into the styrofoam bait bucket. The youngest boy's small hand in there, massaging many worms at once.

You made it sound so simple, Sarah says. The way men fight. Easy. With a drink to follow-up.

That's how it seemed at the time.

At the time you were half-dead with bourbon.

Silas casts his own line, the hook sailing out and falling precisely, a tiny anchor. You never seem like someone who needs taking care of.

I wish we had scissors, Sarah says to Ruby, who has lost her bait, possibly on purpose.

Why? Ruby says, pinching.

Sarah turns back to Silas. It always surprised me, you know. Every time. Because we had fights, lots of fights, that stopped with screaming. She forces the worm onto Ruby's hook, throws her wrist and hands the line back: Now pull it in nice and slow. The fish need to see your worm swimming along.

Minding his own business, Ruby says.

He was a strong enough guy for his size, Silas says.

Men are, Sarah says.

It probably would have been much worse if you hadn't fought back.

Well I did, Sarah says. I mean, you stop fighting when you don't care. She straightens her back and leans out. What's that?

What's what?

Here. There's something in the water.

You'll tip the boat.

I won't. You lean the other way. It's a rod. Sarah throws a quick glance over the children. Did we lose a rod? She dips a hand into the water and grabs a blue fishing rod out by the handle. There's a long line on it and she reels in quickly, pulling in a shining, slapping bass, sixteen or seventeen inches.

Mommy! Ruby drops her own rod in her lap. You caught my fish!

Silas pulls his body to one side to steady the boat. Jesus, he says. Only you could accidentally catch a bass. We're losing the light. He pulls a small pipe from his breast pocket. Will you take a hoot?

Sarah lets the bass land against her feet, wet and thrashing. Gestures at the kids.

Right, Silas says. Don't tell Glenna.

I'm more used to close quarters than you are.

So I've heard. You can't even manage a wank. Silas brings the pipe up close with one hand, sparks a lighter with the other. He breathes out and Sarah catches the scent, sweet and charry, but shakes her head.

I manage, she says. But I don't smoke anymore. She picks up the squirming fish and places it in Ruby's lap. He looks just like he's breathing, doesn't he, she says, showing Ruby where the gills are throbbing open. When really he can't breathe at all. Really he's choking.

Silas reaches the pipe toward her and Sarah leaves her hands where they are, on the fish.

The problem is it gives me this intense sense of well-being, she says.

Well, we can't have that.

Really, Sarah says. I can't. It makes it so I can't write.

Because you're not miserable? Silas takes another haul on the pipe, tosses the lighter back in his pocket.

Because I stop asking questions.

What do we do with him now? Ruby says.

We give him a name, Sarah says. And then we throw him back in.

They pull the boat hard up onto shore, Ruby and the boys with wet legs, wading in.

My mommy caught a fish *and* a new fishing rod! Ruby yells to Glenna's mother. She's been waiting to corral the children. There's a fire going at the other end of the beach, Glenna holding Ilsa's baby and Ilsa beckoning to the waders with marshmallows. Sarah lets go of Ruby's hand, walks up to the house. In the kitchen she pours a scotch and fills the sink.

What are you doing? Silas in the doorway.

No one's touched these, Sarah says, lifting a stack of dirty plates into the water. She doesn't want to say, There's only so much happy family I can take. Squeezes out a measure of dish soap and starts in, cutlery first. Silas picks up her glass and holds it to the light, squinting.

Beckett. I'm so bored. He puts the glass down and leans against the counter.

Then go out to the fire, Sarah says.

You know what I mean.

Sarah rubs at her nose with the sudsy back of her hand, then shakes the soap off into the water. I want to be your friend, she says.

So be my friend. Silas standing there with a green-checked tea towel in his hand. Be my friend, Beckett.

You have everything, Sarah says.

When he leaves she can hear Glenna outside the screen door, pulling him down toward the fire.

Hey, Silas says.

Where the hell are you, Glenna says.

Later Sarah finishes her scotch by the bonfire, and another besides. The men get into the bourbon. She's the last woman standing, all the others in bed or tending babies. Just one shot, Silas begs and she lets him follow her up to the house. He's drunk and holds onto her fingers as they walk inside. He wants to be led by the hand, his fingers curved around hers.

Ruby's hand when I'm walking her to bed, Sarah thinks. When it's dark.

The back of his hand is coarse with short, jutting hairs. Sarah is seized by an urge to squeeze it reassuringly, squeeze until the bones bend and break.

He pours the last of the bourbon into camp mugs.

My wife doesn't like me when you're around, he says.

Sarah picks up her tin mug and twirls, landing unsteadily, one hand on the kitchen counter to stop herself.

Your wife thinks I'm teenager of the year.

Shh, Silas says. You'll wake up the whole house.

Sarah takes herself for a little walk along the counter. I had a house, she says. Remember my house?

It was a great house! Silas lifts his mug in homage to her house.

I know! It was great! We were so great. Everyone thought we were so great. She stops and points a finger at Silas. You think I don't want all this? The finger gyrates, indicating the room, the house. Silas isn't sure. I already did it, Sarah says. She steps forward and lands the finger in the middle of his chest.

I figured we'd be old on a porch, all that garbage, she says. You know how many times I asked him?

To marry you. Silas grabs her mug and takes a sip.

To stop fucking it up.

They drink and Sarah pulls him into the pantry. He's soft, with downy shoulders under his shirt. She doesn't kiss him, but falls to the floor and takes his cock into her mouth and lets the tip slide back against her throat. He tastes the way she expects him to taste: like sweat and sleep and especially urine. When she pulls back he drops down to meet her. She lets him go-to, as though this were his idea, pushing her onto her back, pressing down into her shoulders, one hand pulling at her shorts.

From the floor what she can see is the winter-store: jam

and flour, oats, pickles, coffee, rice. Supplies for a reliable place, somewhere to raise children and feed them, fix things that are broken, keep on. The jars and sacks of meal are steady as pictures on the walls, not a permanent record but markers for some future.

Silas presses his mouth on hers. She lets him. It's more or less the same as any other, hard and burnt by alcohol, but when she moves him between her legs he pulls up, giggling, and she can see that he's afraid of her. A sudden memory of another man, also married: when she was eighteen, the sputter of candles in her university residence bedroom. For three months he held her head, wrapped her hand around his cock, but left her clothes on. Told her, I can't be unfaithful. You know how I feel.

She pushes Silas away. The two of them sitting there on the pantry floor and her foot against the bottom of the shelf. A jar falls and lands with a thud. It cracks, rather than sending shards across the room. The sticky insides somehow catch the glass before it has time to smash. Smithereens, Sarah thinks.

She's on her feet, Silas still down on the ground. Beckett, he says. You have pine needles on your bum. This is meant to sound boyish. Threat over. Sarah shoves her shirt into her waistband.

You'd better clean that up, she says, and points to the jam jar. And put your dick away. Your wife is waiting for you.

She walks up to the bunkhouse and he doesn't follow. The beam of the flashlight through the screen. Ruby pulls herself awake. Sarah turns the light off, swishes each foot in the water bucket and opens the door.

There are twenty bears per square kilometre here, Ruby

195

says and closes her eyes again.

Sarah undresses quickly and sits down on the edge of the bed. Their clothes, hers and Ruby's, in a tangle on the floor.

There's a pillow shoved up along the wall that could almost be a body. Sliding into bed with him, faceless him, his blond beard: Sarah thinks of this. The way you can sleep with someone who's been your friend for a long time. The kind of talk, or the quiet fucking reserved for hotel rooms, baby asleep next to you in the collapsible crib.

Well. Sarah thinks. Do you wait. Do we whisper to each other: Hi Honey how was your day. Your hand up inside my shirt, the newspaper falling aside, do we let it turn dirty. Do you wait?

She pulls back the sheets. Her notebook. Switches on the little book-light. Ruby's breath comes soft and even. There's the nearly-full moon, out on the lake, the screaming loons. In the water bucket by the front door, a white moth.

ACKNOWLEDGMENTS

There are many people to thank. First, my editor, Stan Dragland, who fixed everything, and Michael Winter, who got me started on stories in the first place. The Banff Centre for the Arts for giving me a place to get started and Pasha Malla for his insight. Kim Jernigan and the whole *New Quarterly* for being my best friends in the short story game. Sam Haywood for her vote of confidence. My list of indentured readers: Heather Colquhoun, Nancy Jo Cullen, Matthew Henderson, Leigh Nash, Meaghan Strimas, Carey Toane. Jill Wigmore more than any of these. Robbie and Nic and Megan at Invisible for being so damn great. My parents for running backup. George Murray, who came in late, but who probably suffered more than most.

I am grateful to the Ontario Arts Council, whose funding made writing this book possible.

Many of these stories were first published in one form or another in the following magazines: *The New Quarterly, The Fiddlehead, This Magazine*, and *The Puritan*. I'm very lucky.

Niko Tinbergen's essay, "The Bee-Hunters of Hulshorst", which I found in *The Norton Reader, Sixth Edition* (1965), was very valuable to the writing of my story *Field Work*.

INVISIBLE PUBLISHING is committed to working with writers who might not ordinarily be published and distributed commercially. We work exclusively with emerging and under-published authors to produce entertaining, affordable books.

We believe that books are meant to be enjoyed by everyone and that sharing our stories is important. In an effort to ensure that books never become a luxury, we do all that we can to make our books more accessible.

We are collectively organized and our production processes are transparent. At Invisible, publishers and authors recognize a commitment to one another, and to the development of communities which can sustain and encourage storytellers.

If you'd like to know more please get in touch.
info@invisiblepublishing.com

Invisible Publishing
Halifax & Toronto